July 5, 2017

To John,

Enjoy the novel, my main man. Thank you for your constant support & friendship! God Bless & Go Canes,

Alex Mor

Phil. 4:13

Wolfpack

Wolfpack

A Novel by

Alex Montoya

To order additional copies of this book, contact:
Xlibris
1-888-795-4274
www.Xlibris.com
Orders@Xlibris.com
757145

Contents

Dedication

Dedicated to my families in Colombia and the United States

and to my Wolfpack.

Wolfpack: Introduction

A lot can happen in a year.

This novel was created after a particularly tumultuous year experienced by some friends and I. We lost love. We lost jobs. We lost hope. But what struck me was what we still had: each other. Although we weren't necessarily friends *because* of our losses – my Wolfpack in San Diego, like most groups, had different ways of meeting each other – we absolutely carried each other through tough times.

After realizing the special bond we had formed, I asked each of them if I could base a character on their experiences. Each one said yes and I promised to change enough things to where no reader could properly identify which character was based on which real-life person. Such a caveat is necessary in beautiful San Diego – at once it's a large city and a small town.

The "Wolfpack" paradigm is based on the New Millenium film trilogy, *The Hangover*. Those characters proudly identify themselves as a Wolfpack, so much so that it became a part of American pop culture lexicon. The similarities to the film end there, however (minus one chapter occurring in Las Vegas).

But since we're on the subject of American cinema or celebrities, when you read this novel, you can imagine the primary characters as follows:

Fernando Guzman – Enrique Iglesias
Katie McDonald – Gwyneth Paltrow / Reese Witherspoon
Teddy Jackson – Taye Diggs

Liz Wong – Lisa Ling
Jenn Holtz – Margot Robbie
Jack Murphy – Michael Rappaport

If you know those actors, great, but if not, even better – you can envision the character in your mind's eye. Aside from those imaginative guides, each character was 100% created as fiction, a composite of various people I've known.

Some cities and famous people and landmarks and establishments are real. However, the narratives are all fictitious, as is each storyline. In other words, I didn't see any of this with my eye, only my mind's eye.

Thank you to the I-CAN Center, a computer lab for people with disabilities in the downtown branch of the San Diego Public Library, and to Xlibris Publishing, for providing the platforms for my creativity. Thank you to my Father above, and to all my family and friends, especially my Wolfpack, for supporting this endeavor. This is my first, after three self-help books, novel. I do hope you enjoy it.

Keep Inspiring,
Alex Montoya,
Author

Chapter 1

Almost Paradise

Fernando & Katie

"It was the best of times, it was the worst of times..."

The room erupted with laughter, a mixture of gleeful mirth and good-natured groaning.

"Oh, come on, be serious!" pleaded Katie, placing the palm of her hand on her boyfriend Fernando's sweater, a combination of a love-tap and stern admonishment. The sweater wasn't just a sweater, it was of the Christmas-ugly-sweater variety, complete with a Santa Clause stitched onto the chest, pulling on several reindeer, Rudolph's nose and Santa's outfit adorned in bright red fabrics. And Fernando wasn't just Katie's boyfriend, he was her fiancée.

"Okay, okay, okay, okay," Fernando said in rapid-fire speed, "I'll make a good toast. This is serious, this is serious."

Katie rolled her eyes and took a sip of her wine.

"Wait, don't drink yet," Fernando said, "I have to make a toast first!"

"Well get on with it!" Katie responded, in a more agitated tone.

"Come on Freddy, you can do this." The verbal encouragement came from somewhere in the crowd of partygoers assembled in Fernando and Katie's downtown San Diego condominium. Being called Freddy actually startled him. It was a nickname he'd owned since childhood but it suddenly dawned upon him that he hadn't been called that in his home in months.

Since…when? Since that magical night in Disneyland, almost one year ago, that he knelt in front of the Sleeping Beauty castle and proposed?

Was that weird that Fernando noticed Katie hadn't endearingly called him Freddy in months? Was that a bad thing? Why would he even take note of such an anomaly?

Well, no time to reflect on that now. This was *their* Christmas party – *I don't want the invitations to say holiday party,* Katie had emphasized, *it's a Christmas party* – in *their* apartment, overlooking the canopy of blue skies, a glittering bayside and endless supply of gleaming daytime sunshine and evening stars buffeting the horizon. He had asked her to move in after six months of dating but she answered with an abbreviated but strong Beyonce dance routine, saying in sing-song fashion that *If you like it / Than you shoulda put a ring on it.*

So he did. At Disneyland on a chilly winter night. She ecstatically said yes. Now they were co-residents. Hosting a *Christmas* party for 20 assembled, tipsy, raucous guests, bedecked in blazers and cocktail dresses, nary another ugly sweater in sight. Katie noticed that too, and expressed her annoyance with Fernando's attire earlier in the evening.

He raised his wine glass aloft once more, bellowing: "It was the best of times! It was the worst of times! But through it all in 2015, you've been there with us. So here's a toast, to you….

to us….

and may you wake up feeling….

like you've been hit by a bus!

Salud!"

Saluuuuuud! The room burst into a cacophony of glasses clanking and voices cackling, Fernando's impromptu twisting of Dickens eliciting great laughter.

Fernando laughed too, forgetting to toast the glass of the fiancée next to him. That increased her displeasure and she sighed as she took a sip, and then a gulp, from her goblet.

This is ridiculous, she thought to herself, I need to step outside for some fresh air and get away from these immature animals.

What Is Your Problem?

Katie grabbed a coat that was hanging near the front door, before she realized she didn't even know if that was *her* jacket. Oh well, she thought, I actually just need to step outside for a few minutes so any coat will do. Glancing behind her to see if Fernando was trailing – he wasn't – Katie threw on the tan pea-coat and strode toward the apartment door. Closing it behind her firmly, she continued her strident pace down the hallway that led to the elevator.

A man was walking in the opposite direction, the DING of the elevator indicating he had just exited it. Walking past each other in the narrow hallway, their shoulders brushed. They both said the same thing: "Excuse me!" Except he, an impeccably dressed African-American gentleman, said it out of genuine concern and slight embarrassment. Katie's *excuse me* was brusque, an acknowledgement that she had bumped him but not really an apology.

That didn't sit well with him. Instantly he asked, "Hey, what is your problem?"

The words stopped Katie like a fire alarm or a DO NOT ENTER sign. She halted. Spinning around to face her inquisitor and tossing her blond hair aside, she took two steps closer to him.

"Excuse me?" she repeated, except in question form.

The man was surprised. So he re-stated *his* question: "What IS your problem?"

Katie chuckled and looked down at her expensive Jimmy Choo high heels. She then looked intently at her sudden hallway companion. Clearing her throat, she asked, "Uh, what's your name, sir?"

"Teddy, uh, Ted. Ted. Jackson," he stammered.

"Oh. Teddy? Ted? Mr. Jackson?" replied Katie, clearly relishing the man's surprising nervousness, "Do you wanna KNOW what my problem is?"

He had asked but now he didn't want to know. Teddy could tell this was not a rhetorical question. The feisty blonde was going to respond anyway.

"Do you wanna KNOW what my problem is?" She edged closer to him.

"I'll tell you what my problem is," Kate intoned, digging a well-manicured finger into his silk blue tie. "My problem…is….MEN!"

With that she spun back around and walked angrily to the elevator. Teddy Jackson stood still, awkwardly, until he could hear the simultaneous DING of the elevator and the lady's high heels clasping against the floor, indicating she had entered the elevator. The doors closed with a WHOOSH.

"Wow!" he exclaimed, before lowering his voice to a whisper. "*White women!*"

Shaking his head, he walked away, to his apartment down the hall and around the corner. On the way he passed what sounded like a lively party.

A man stepped out, suddenly blurting, "Hey! Did you see a…?"

Teddy smirked. Pointing to the elevator entryway, he replied, "Yeah, man. She went THAT way. Good luck with that."

The elevator doors opened and immediately Fernando saw what he thought he'd see and *hoped* he'd see. Katie was near the edge of the building's rooftop, leaning against a small wall that allowed her to rest her elbows on it and gaze into the glitter of the stars and downtown lights.

"Don't jump," Fernando chuckled.

With an exasperated sigh, Katie quickly turned to face him and then turned outwardly to the city again. "How did you know I was here?" she asked.

"Well, a guy in the hallway told me you took the elevator," he explained, "and I know this is, like, your happy place so….wait….are you *smoking*?"

Quickly, Katie removed the cigarette from her lips, as if her father had caught her taking a puff, which made her even more irritated that she did that so rapidly. That cigarette had tasted *good*.

"For your information, this is NOT my happy place," Katie said, "I just come here when I need to think and ponder and get away. And I'm only smoking because I found these cigarettes and matches in this girl's jacket. I don't even know whose jacket this *is*. I only smoke if I'm stressed. You should know that."

Turning back to Fernando, she asked, "Do you even *know* me?"

Did he *know* her? The question was as silly as it was injurious. Fernando felt hurt and amused simultaneously. He knew Katie McDonald as well as he knew himself.

And knowing himself was not an uncomplicated endeavor.

Fernando Hernan Guzman was born in the Central Valley of California, near Bakersfield. He was named not after a relative or iconic religious figure, but after a baseball player. In 1981, Fernando Valenzuela took Major League Baseball – and the entire sporting world – by storm when he came from a tiny town, a village really, in Mexico and blew away opposing batters for the Los Angeles Dodgers. Valenzuela won the National League Rookie of the Year and Cy Young Award – bestowed to the league's top pitcher – but to migrant farmworker Rogelio Guzman in Bakersfield, it was about more than winning hardware.

Fernando Valuenzuela brought *hope*. Hope that Rogelio's favorite team could erase its stained past of pushing out residents, mostly Latinos, out of Chavez Ravine so that Dodger Stadium could be erected there. Hope that the *Doyers* could finally topple the Big Red Machine of Cincinnati and the mighty New York Yankees. Hope that a Mexican could come to the United States and succeed in making all his dreams come true.

So in 1986, after Valenzuela had completed over five seasons of dominant screwball superiority, Rogelio and his wife Ines had their first baby. Naturally, the beaming father wanted to name him after the pitcher that performed so well, the national media gave his fervent following a moniker: *Fernandomania*. Ines understood and obliged.

As a boy, his father would give young Fernando a summer job that was a glimpse into Papa's daily work. Rogelio Guzman was a year-round farmworker who picked fruits and vegetables from a local field. It was a brutal living, one that exposed him and his shift workers to chilling cold in the winter, rain-soaked mud in the winter, and oppressive heat in the summer.

Summertime was when Fernando experienced his father's daily vocation. From June through August, he helped pick strawberries, enduring the pain of constant stooping and abrasions on his hands and legs. From grade school through high school, this was his summer existence. He hated it but he knew his family needed it because eventually he had two younger siblings.

He hated it and his father was glad he hated it.

"This is not the life for you," Rogelio would tell his son at the family dinner table. "Don't follow in my footsteps. Get your education. Start a career in an office somewhere. Bending over, day after day, poking holes in your fingers and hands and legs. I do it so someday you won't *have* to."

Fernando nodded silently. His mother gave both father and son plastic tubs in which to soak their battered feet. They recuperated while eating tacos, beans, and rice, and drank flavorful *horchata*. Once Hernan gave his near-nightly reminder that being a farmworker, or engaging in any type of manual labor, really, was not the future he envisioned for any of his kids, conversation turned to baseball.

The 1990s were just like the previous two decades for Rogelio: Dodgers baseball playing on a small counter-top radio, Vin Scully broadcasting the action in lyrical perfection, with the boys in blue battling the Reds or Giants or Astros for National League West supremacy. Fernando Guzman's namesake, Fernando Valenzuela, was still baffling batters and sustaining strikeouts. In 1990, in fact, he pitched a no-hitter at Dodger Stadium, almost a full decade into his career.

"Freddy," Rogelio had intoned that night after the game concluded, "you just remember what we heard tonight. Anything is possible. Fernando Valenzuela isn't so young anymore, he even needs glasses. And he pitched a no-hitter. *Increible*."

Nights like Valenzuela's no-no, or even lectures administered by his father at the dinner table, or in their old, beat-up pickup truck, would sometimes pop into Fernando Guzman's head. Sometimes these memories were triggered by seeing televised images of Fernando, the pitcher, now firmly ensconced in the Dodgers broadcast booth. Or he would hear a phrase like *Si Se Puede* and instantly his mind flashed to his father firmly but encouragingly tell him, "*Si se puede*. Yes you can."

It was an old United Farm Workers chant promulgated by Cesar Chavez, a farmworker who became a civil rights and union rights icon. Fernando's father had marched alongside Chavez in protests that helped secure fair pay and working conditions for *campesinos* – camp workers – like Rogelio Guzman. He would regale his eldest boy with tales of marching with Chavez, and listening to folk singers like Ramon "Chunky" Sanchez, and working endlessly for better pay and dignity. The stories all ended the same, though: *I am proud to be a farm worker. But I do this so you don't have to. Get your education. And be somebody's boss!*

It instilled in Fernando a diligent work ethic throughout high school, college, and law school. While an undergraduate at the University of Southern California, he had the same get-a-great-job-and-fancy-car goals as his classmates, but his ambition was deeper. Neither of his parents had above a fourth grade education. Certainly his father couldn't pick strawberries forever; all the years of stooping had already caused interminable back pain. The faithful son had to ensure his parents had a financially safe future.

Because of that, he was a planner, a builder, and someone always restlessly looking into the future.

What mattered right now was the present. He had a wonderful, high-salaried job in a well-respected law firm, and impressive condo, in this most gorgeous city of San Diego, but none of that mattered as much as the sight of his fiancée, cold and shivering, smoking someone else's cigarettes, in a fit of unhappiness.

Fernando was forthright but tread carefully. Placing one arm around to provide instant warmth, he asked, "Katie, what's wrong?"

"I don't know, Freddie, it's..." her voice trailed off as she hid her face in her gloved hands. "It's *everything*. Your toast seemed so silly, and I don't even know half the people in that party, and I have to start wedding planning soon, and I just..."

"Whoa, whoa, whoa," he interjected, "babe, calm down, relax. So my toast wasn't very good. I get it. I guess I got a little silly."

Fernando admitted, too, that he overextended the guest list and invited people from work, USC, the gym, essentially every social community he was a part of. But he was confused by her wedding-planning reticence.

"Babe, you're going to be *great* at wedding planning," Fernando said while holding her face in both of his hands now, "and it's not just going to be you. It's going to be *us*. We're in this together."

Katie knew everything Fernando was saying was true, but it just didn't make her feel any better. She had this gloom, this unhappiness that pervaded her like one of those perpetually overcast San Diego cloudy days in early summer. June Gloom the weather forecasters on television called it.

Her mother had warned her about this. *Katherine Jacqueline McDonald*, her mother once said, *you see problems where there are none. Appreciate what you have. Keep your feelings to yourself – some things just cause more trouble than they're worth.*

That was part of Katie's Irish-Catholic upbringing in suburban Chicago. Girls went to college ostensibly to earn a degree but also find a man to marry. It was bad enough, her parents said, she took that business degree from Notre Dame and accepted a job offer all the way across the country in San Diego. But she redeemed – they actually used that word, *redeemed* – herself by finding a nice young lad to marry, even if Fernando had attended Notre Dame's archrival school, USC.

At times Katie's voice still had a Chicago, Midwest twang to it. "Oh my *gash*, Freddy, I don't know. I know what's wrong with me," she began sobbing into his arms.

"It's ok, it's ok," he said soothingly, "it's…it's nerves. You're gonna be fine. You've got your maid of honor lined up, you've got your bridesmaids, you're gonna be an absolutely stunning bride. It's gonna be great. Everything's gonna be great. But TONIGHT, we don't worry about anything. We're gonna drink and feast and have a marvelous time."

Katie couldn't deny that a Christmas party – unless it was a Festivus party made famous in old *Seinfeld* episodes for their "airing of grievances" – was the improper place to discuss, or even think about, her doubts.

She didn't doubt Fernando was a fantastic guy. She knew that when mutual friends introduced them at the University of San Diego. He was in law school and she was getting her MBA. He was tall, handsome, and had the subtle gift of speaking convincingly without making one feel they were in the middle of an attorney's closing argument.

Katie had met Fernando's parents and saw where he derived his blue-collar, hard-scrabble ways. His liberal, blue-state political views didn't mesh with her rock-ribbed Republican background. But, heck, that didn't bug her as much as the fact he graduated from 'SC. Football Saturdays were tense in the fall. But he was funny, generous, and romantic. When he asked her on a date to go paddle boarding, she was intrigued. After three dates elicited a first kiss, she was thrilled.

Then when the absurdly perfect night at Disneyland occurred, a night that couldn't be more flawless had she planned it herself, Katie was overjoyed. She had ditched her parents' expectations of finding a husband at Notre Dame but ended up finding one in Southern California. Her parents, Tom and Marjorie, met him and *loved* him. Katie elicited the same reaction from Fernando's parents. Both sets of parents were happy. Fernando was always beaming. All close friends were happy and approving.

Why, then, did Katie McDonald feel so unhappy?

Those thoughts would have to be stifled for now. Fernando kissed Katie's forehead and led her gently back toward the elevators. A Christmas party awaited. There were guests to hug, pecks on the cheek to be administered, and countless bottles of wine to receive. Katie knew how to play the role of consummate social host.

She could *do* this. But shouldn't she feel a level of elation, hosting a Christmas party with her beloved fiancée? Why was she unhappy? Not just tonight, but in general – why did every day leave a feeling of discontentedness?

She knew it.

Fernando knew it.

Katie wasn't exactly shy at hiding her feelings – about anything. Things she didn't like – dogs in sweaters, for example – or things she very much enjoyed. Like country music or movies filled with romantic and dramatic storylines. Fernando was bored to tears by country western *and* love stories.

But was her unhappiness simply related to the two of them having divergent hobbies or likes and dislikes?

Or was it something…deeper?

"Freddie, we need to t…" Katie began.

But Fernando merely pressed his index finger against his lips. *Shhhhhh!*

"Let's go enjoy this party," he said. "People are waiting on us. Let's show them a good time. Whatever you want to talk about, we can take care of after the party, ok?"

Katie nodded affirmatively.

They had a Christmas party to get back to.

Chapter 2

Bea Happy

Beatriz Feliz

As Fernando Guzman and Katie McDonald, the not-so-happily-engaged couple returned to their Christmas party inside Fernando's condominium, another couple was leaving. Katie didn't recognize them at all, and Fernando barely did, but he acted like he knew them well and that their leaving wounded him.

"Heyyyyy, you're leaving?" he bemoaned.

"Yes, we have to go. Fernando, I'm not sure if you remember meeting me," said a brunette, in her mid-30's, with mid-length hair, "but I'm Beatriz Feliz, and this is my husband, Jose."

The two couples exchanged names and handshakes, with Fernando never admitting he did not know how or where they had previously met.

"You and I met at the Hispanic Chamber of Commerce networking mixer a couple weeks ago," Beatriz said, as if she could read Fernando's mind, "and you invited me to your party when you found out my husband and I only live a couple blocks away."

Fernando grinned because, well, that *sounded* like something he would do.

"And please, my friends call me 'Bea'," she continued. "Anyways, we have a sitter but Jose said he'd like to go home to the kids."

Jose smiled sheepishly, but curiously did not say anything else.

"Well thank you for coming, Bea and Jose," Katie interjected. "Uh, Bea, what is it you said you did?"

"Oh, I work in marketing, for the Gilmore Group," she responded, and in one motion, like a magician wielding an ace of spades, had two business cards ready to present to Katie and Fernando.

"Marketing, public relations, advertising, we do a little bit of everything over at our shop," Bea said proudly.

Jose sighed. "That's my wife, always networking."

"Well that's the name of the game, isn't it?" she said, though more so to Katie and Fernando, and not really directing her answer to her husband. "Besides, networking is what got us invited to this fabulous party. And it *really* was a fabulous party, thank you."

Bea Feliz was a product of cross-border Southern California. Her parents were born in Guadalajara, Mexico and moved to San Diego in the late 1970's. In 1986 President Reagan issued a sweeping amnesty law allowing any undocumented immigrants to file for United States citizenship. Hugo and Maria Feliz signed up for it and dreamed of a better future for their baby girl, Beatriz.

Though they had left behind their native land and found jobs mostly in manual labor – he in construction and she in housekeeping – their message to their only child was unmistakable. This is a land of opportunity. Get a good education to fully take advantage of that. Yet never, ever forget the motherland and the fierce pride of being a Mexican.

Bea was, of course, too young to truly remember or know Guadalajara, but she would spend parts of summers visiting family there. Simply being in the tequila capital of the world gave her keen insight that her bilingualism was a weapon. She could move freely throughout Guadalajara and nearby regions and then return home to captivate her English-speaking friends with stories of beautiful festivals, serenading mariachis, and the most scrumptious foods ever consumed.

She listened to her parents and earned her college degree at San Diego State University. Without trying, really, the rest fell in lockstep. She had secretly always dreamed of attending college somewhere back East, where ivy covered the campus walls and leaves lazily drifted about in the autumn. But if that had happened, maybe she wouldn't have landed the coveted summer marketing internship that led to a job straight out of college.

Beatriz had her Business Administration and Marketing degree from SDSU and her parents were certainly proud, but her *Mama* wanted to know when she'd be settling down. So she started dating Jose, the only other Latino at the firm, and within two years they were married. Then her mom started clamoring for grandkids and although Jose said he wanted "to wait a while," they had two kids in the next four years – Gabriela and Maximiliano. They quickly doted on little Gabby and Max.

The 20's are a whirlwind for most people and so it was for Bea. Except instead of nights going to clubs or fantastic vacations, weekends were spent shuttling the kids to soccer practice and summers were for educational trips to the aquarium and World Famous San Diego Zoo.

"Bea, slow down, let's maybe take a vacation for ourselves," Jose would occasionally plead. But she would hear none of it, proudly reminding him that she balanced career and family and was perfectly happy. Wasn't *he*?

Although their condo was modest, it was large enough to also house Bea's parents, guaranteeing she always had built-in babysitters and life advice. As the kids got bigger, perhaps they could afford to move to a suburb somewhere but the cost of housing in San Diego was enormous.

"This is why we should take a vacation *now*," Jose urged, "before all our resources are taken in some house somewhere."

Bea sensed in her husband a yearning for adventure, which is why invitations to parties or couples-nights were so valued. But that also made it peculiar as to why, on this night where they could stay out 'till dawn if desired, all Jose wanted to do was get back home. It made no sense.

Thus far she had done everything right in life. While many of her girlfriends spent their college years in fraternity houses and long weekends in Cabo, Beatriz dutifully spent nights in the library or volunteering at orphanages in Tijuana. Her degree was hard-earned. Her husband was smooth and smart. Her kids were brilliant, Gabby having already won a county spelling bee and Max successfully winning a junior science competition. She was a top producer at the Gilmore Group, her bosses loved her, and her Spanish fluency gave her company access to international clientele. She dutifully took care of her parents. She made dinner every night and never missed a yoga class on weekends.

Responsibility, family, satisfaction – Beatriz Feliz had it all! Some days she even had to remind herself to step away from her day-planner – she still preferred carrying one around to supplement her iPhone, which was always buzzing with texts, Tweets, and appointment notices – just to say thanks.

This is the life she wanted. Bustling with career, family, and self-fulfillment. From the moment she awoke to when she would fall asleep at night reading a self-help book, Bea's every hour was accounted for. And it all felt so good.

As they left the Christmas party, she grabbed Jose's arm a little tighter.

"Tell you what," she said, "why don't we take a little detour and go grab some coffee first?"

"Are you sure it's part of the schedule?" he asked with a smirk.

The question startled her.

Bea punched Jose in the arm. "Yes, it's part of the schedule – although there is no *schedule!*" she insisted.

"Let's be spontaneous, let's be fun, let's get some coffee!" she urged.

Chuckling, Jose replied, "Ok, let's go get some coffee. Maybe we can discuss taking a vacation. No kids, no parents, just us."

Bea pretended not to hear the last part. "Oh look, there's a coffee shop up ahead! Let's go!"

Onward they marched, into the frosty December night.

It's Over

The days leading up to Christmas are so many things. Joyful. Cheerful. Harried. Pressured.

It's all around: the music, the store advertising, Christmas cards hung in homes and businesses alike. During the month of December (if not before that), there are constant reminders that 'tis the season.

Fernando loved this time of year. He worked hard and was generally frugal, so he could afford to lavish his loved ones with gifts. It also represented a sort of status achievement, that he had made it this far and could generously bestow gifts on everyone from his parents to his younger siblings to his housekeeper.

The tricky part, though, was what present should he buy for his fiancée? He had already asked Katie to move in with him, and frequently gave her presents as mundane as oil changes to as fancy as candlelit dinners atop downtown's famed University Club. The biggest gift of all, course, rested on her finger in the form of the engagement ring he had presented at Disneyland.

Everything a woman could want, Fernando had given Katie. Stability, material possessions, even impromptu weekend getaways to Santa Barbara or Catalina Island. Her mother often reminded her how fortunate she was. Her friends constantly expressed envy at her luck.

So why then, with just a week before Christmas, were they here in Fernando's black Lexus, in his parking garage? They had been invited to a dinner that night with Fernando's boss. Only three other couples had been invited, people who were either partners at the firm or were on the fast track to doing so. The dinner was at a dazzling Italian restaurant, the kind where you have to put proper *oomph* into saying the name. It dripped with sophistication.

At dinner Katie had hardly said a word. Between copious amounts of wine and the attorneys laughing themselves silly over current and past cases – names and storylines which bore no familiarity or interest to her – she found no place to contribute.

Occasionally Fernando would nudge her to coax a laugh out of her, and Katie would dutifully smile. But otherwise she was just *bored*.

Was this her future? Dinners with partners and clients where the conversation focused solely on the main principals? Spouses and significant others weren't really a *part* of the conversation, they were window dressing, a laugh track to the banter.

"Katie, you hardly said a word at dinner," Fernando said as he parked the car.

In response she only mustered a shrug.

"Is everything ok?" he asked.

Katie remained silent.

"Well, just remember tomorrow we have brunch with our neighbors, the Costellos, and then I wanted to finish up some Christmas shopping, so I thought you and I could do it together. Because remember, Monday night we have…."

"I want out."

Katie's words pierced the night air.

Fernando wasn't sure what she meant. He asked, "You want out? You wanna get out of the car?"

He unbuckled his seatbelt so he could prepare to get out, go to her side of the car, and let her out.

"No, Freddy," she said firmly. Looking him directly in the eyes, she said, "I want…I need…to get out of this relationship."

Fernando froze. He earnestly didn't know whether to cry or laugh, not the type of laughter of amusement but of sheer absurdity. Really he was mortified.

Silence filled the car. Both could hear their cell phones whirring with notifications of text messages and incoming e-mails. In the background another car had slammed its trunk door shut.

"I want out," Katie repeated.

"I heard you," Fernando responded, his stare intently fixed on Katie in the passenger seat.

"I heard you," he said, "but….I'm not…believing…what I'm hearing."

Katie took a deep breath. "Fernando, I've been unhappy for a long time. And I know this is lousy timing, but look, you give me all these things, and they're great. But I'm still unhappy. I'm still unhappy."

Fernando could feel his anger rising, so he broke into a nervous laugh while saying, "This is a joke, right? A sick joke? I've given you everything…"

"Yes, I know, you've given me everything," Katie said testily. "But there needs to be more, Freddy. I should be *excited* about our relationship, excited for our future. It's like it's all scripted, it's all laid out the way my parents said it should be, and the way *your* parents said it should be. They're happy. You're happy. But no one ever asks if *I'm* happy."

"Are you happy, Katie?" Fernando asked, with a tone of defiance.

"No," she said flatly, "I'm not."

For all of his expertise in cross-examining witnesses, Fernando was at a loss for words. Any afterglow remaining from the dinner had left him. He was thunderstruck.

Katie unlocked her car door. "I've been wanting to say something for a long time, but I just couldn't figure out how. I'm sorry. I'll collect some of my things tonight. It's over."

There were no other words that needed to be said. A million questions ran through Fernando's mind but he was too shocked, too exhausted, to ask them. For all the frequent spats he and Katie would get into, he figured she was too sensitive and he was too hard-headed. But the notion of them splitting never entered his mind.

Was this a twisted joke? Would Katie come to her senses inside the apartment?

Yet, for how taken aback he was, a part of him knew. A part of him saw this coming. Maybe not to the point of a full-fledged break-up but he could see this coming. He could see Katie's dissatisfaction. He tried to ignore it. He tried to bury it in presents and parties and social engagements. Katie was now...gone?

Say It Isn't So

Well *this* was a surprise. Jose Feliz never scheduled impromptu lunch dates. Lunches were normally eaten at his desk. That's the way he'd been since Bea met him at the Gilmore Group before he eventually moved on to a financial services management firm.

So when he asked her two days prior if she had Friday free for lunch, she was startled. Grabbing her phone and glancing at her calendar, it held no appointments that day. No lunch meetings with clients or focus groups or even any girlfriends for catch-up time.

"I'm free," she said with as much astonishment as it was relief.

"Cool, let's grab lunch," Jose said while tying a Windsor knot into through his tie.

"Oh maybe we can sneak away and grab some presents for the kids," Bea said hurriedly, "I still have one thing to get Max, and Gabby could use another pair of shoes, and I COMPLETELY forgot about the newspaper delivery b..."

"No," Jose said quickly but firmly, "let's just grab lunch, you and me."

At week's end, there they sat, at a Japanese restaurant in downtown San Diego. He didn't order much, save for a couple rolls of sushi. She, on the other hand, was quite hungry and looked forward to devouring some sushi, mitsu soup, teriyaki chicken, and maybe some fried shrimp as a side order.

This is nice, she thought, although maybe she could stretch a few minutes past her lunch hour and buy at least *one* Christmas gift at the nearby mall.

"Honey, I invited you today because we...we...uh...need to talk," Jose said, suddenly fidgeting with his chopsticks.

Bea smiled while responding, "What, is this a meeting? I know, I know I spent too much on gifts already. I'll..."

Jose cut her off. "No. We need to talk about us."

She raised her eyebrows. "About us? What about us? I don't…"

This time Bea interrupted her own sentence. She really didn't know what else to say, or even ask.

Jose took a deep breath. Curiously, ironically, he noticed the overhead sound system was playing Hall & Oates' wistful 1980's pop song about breaking up: *"Say It Isn't So / Ohhh / Oh oh oh"*.

He smiled at the appropriateness of the song for what he was about to say, not a cruel or heartless realization, but certainly an ironic one. It was a dagger to him, he felt, as much as it was about to be to his wife.

"Honey, uh, some things have changed."

She shook her head in confusion, uttering, "Changed? What? Are we in financial trouble?"

"No," Jose responded, glancing around and unable to look his spouse directly in the eyes. Finally, after a few awkward sentences, he just said it all, one big sentence without emotion or hesitation, just to get it out.

"You know I left the Gilmore Group a couple years ago, and things changed, between you and me, we drifted apart, we see each other less, and I, uh, at the new firm, I, well, I've met someone."

Beatriz was still confused but with anger now making the back of her neck feel warm. "You, you, you *met someone?*"

"Yes. I don't really know how to say this but…"

"Just say it. You've met someone?"

"Well, yes. At the new firm, I mean, I know it's not new anymore, but, yes. I met someone. I'm in love with someone else, Beatriz. And I want a divorce."

Bea sat morbidly still, her eyes burning with shock and anger. Jose felt like he'd made his announcement with a megaphone, like the entire restaurant had heard it, but of course no one had.

If I'm being replaced / Say It Isn't Sooo / Oh oh oh…

"Honey, say some…"

"What?" she responded in an angered but whispered voice. "Don't 'honey' me. Don't call me honey. Are you kidding me, Jose?"

Her voice decibel grew and Jose was sure the entire restaurant knew now. A waitress appeared.

She was a slender, porcelain-faced Japanese girl, with a traditional kimono and soft voice. "Is everything ok here? May I get you more soy sauce?"

"No, everything is NOT ok!" Bea snapped at the server.

"Honey," Jose interjected.

"DON'T CALL ME 'HONEY'," she said loudly, before turning to the confused girl. "My husband here just told me he's in love with another woman and wants a divorce!"

The waitress lowered her eyes, not knowing what to say, but knowing not to move. She resembled a *geisha*, ready to serve, but frozen in fear and uncomfortableness.

Bea continued: "You bring me to a restaurant, full of people, the week before Christmas, to tell me, to tell me, *you've met someone?!*"

The waitress slowly, with her head down, edged away from the table, though now indeed there were several onlookers.

"Look, I don't know what to say," Jose said, "I certainly didn't expect this to happen. But I'd be lying if I said I was happy with how our relationship is going."

"It's not a relationship, Jose, it's a *marriage!*"

Jose tried to lower his voice in vain hopes maybe his angered wife would lower hers. "I know it's a marriage, Beatriz, but I'm not happy. I'm living a lie here. And I've met someone who…I'm sorry…I've fallen for someone else. I couldn't go into the New Year living a lie anymore. I'm…I'm sorry."

"Yes you are! You are a sorry excuse for a man!"

With that, Beatriz Feliz stood up, flung her cloth napkin onto the table, and grabbed her glass of water.

SPLASH!!!

The water was flung at Jose's face, which dripped onto his expensive tie, and onto his cashmere blazer. He wiped his face dry, but could not remove the humiliation he now felt.

Bea grabbed her purse and stormed off. Quickly, shock had turned into anger, and anger had turned into plunging pain. She walked briskly past the waitress, who had positioned herself near the hostess stand by the front entrance.

Bea was sobbing now.

Say It Isn't So / Oh oh ohhhh….

Chapter 3

Action Jackson

Teddy "TJ" Jackson

"Sweetie, I told you, sports don't take a holiday. Teams play sports today too and I have to report on it."

One minute, TJ, and we're back on air. The producer's voice intently delivered the message into the earpieces of everyone assembled in the studio – the news anchors, the camera operators, the floor producers.

"Ok, listen, baby, I gotta go. I'll be off by 11:30 and will be right by your side when the ball drops, I promise, ok? Ok, ok, alright, I gotta go…. byeeee."

The three other anchors – a male newscaster with perfectly coiffed hair, a female newscaster with a bright yellow suit, and a weather forecaster who had his suit slightly disheveled to give the impression of I'M WILD, I'M CRAZY, I'M AN ECENTRIC WEATHER GUY – all shot Teddy glances over his long, drawn-out, cooing of 'byeeeeee'.

He hung up his cell phone, switched the setting to silent, and looked back at them. All three television personalities started laughing.

"Oh shut up," said Teddy, to the trio simultaneously, "sometimes my ladies need a little, um, baby talk, ok?"

*And we're on in five, four, three, two, and….*When the floor director flashed her index finger, and the cameras zoomed in on the news desk, it looked like they were having silly banter. In reality, they were laughing at their sportscaster colleague. But anyone watching at home would presume it was an environment of playful kidding and mutual joke-sharing.

They also then cast nervous eyes upon the sports anchor, impeccably dressed in a three-piece dark blue suit, with powder-blue pocket square to match his powder-blue tie. Did he study the newscast script in advance? Or even glance at the teleprompter to see which highlight he would begin narrating? It wasn't unusual for the other on-air talent to make side bets, usually five bucks, about how well Teddy would mask his unpreparedness. Would he say something like, *Tonight, ok, what highlight are we going with here?* Or would he take one cursory peep at the nearby television and base his introduction on whether he saw a football, baseball, soccer ball, basketball, any kind of ball.

Because once he got settled, Teddy made teleprompters as obsolete as captioned headlines. This was *his* show, baby, full of catch-phrases and hip, pop culture references. Sometimes the highlights became secondary. People tuned in to see if the sportscaster in his late 30's would compare LeBron James to comedian Kevin Hart – *"he's everywhere and making money by the millisecond"* – or take verbal jabs at last-place teams, saying, *"the Padres starting rotation is like the Five Heartbeats. Remember them? Don't worry, neither do I."*

Theodore Marvin Jackson, Jr. was born in South Bend, Indiana at the beginning of the 1980's. Already blessed with a last name that matched a famous singing family 90 minutes south in Gary – "Michael was my cousin," he would say, "I got the good looks and he got everything else," – his steel worker father gave him a middle name in honor of crooner Marvin Gaye.

Nicknames alternated for him as easily as he switched hands when carrying a football. He earned an athletic scholarship to Notre Dame, where friends mostly called him "TJ" but fervent Fighting Irish fans dubbed him "Action". Truthfully, he didn't relish the idea of staying in his frigid hometown to play college football – he secretly relished the opportunity of playing in tropical climes like magnificent Miami or luxurious Los Angeles – but his mother made a plea to him. "Stay here for college," she implored him, "it's a world-class education and we can watch you play. I'm a waitress and yo' daddy work in the steel mills. You think we can afford to fly to Flaarda or California to watch you play?"

Teddy Jr. knew his father, a man of few words, would never verbalize such a request. But the proud look on his dad's face when the University of Notre Dame sent a letter offering a paid-in-full scholarship was a look of deepened satisfaction he'd never forget. Teddy not only wanted to make his old man proud, he wanted to give him the joy of watching him score torque-twisting touchdowns and exhibit sizzling speed in person.

Notre Dame was hard, dang hard, academically but Teddy's patience prevailed. He earned his Bachelor's degree in Communications and broke the school record for touchdowns, earning him a spot on the San Francisco 49ers roster. His father saw every touchdown he scored at historic Notre Dame Stadium. His mother, Juanita, would only go to warm-weather games, meaning any game past mid-October Teddy would give his game tickets to an uncle or cousin. But Pops was always in attendance, whether the temperatures were hot, cold, or furiously freezing.

Teddy's professional career was unspectacular, four years with the Niners, followed by a knee injury that led him to parts of three more seasons with Atlanta, Washington, and San Diego. But those initial years in the Bay Area gave him a love for California and his final season in San Diego gave him a sunny locale to permanently call home. He had his Communications degree from Notre Dame, which combined with his charisma and good looks landed him a television gig and even a couple commercial endorsements. Teddy could sell the heck out of a mattress!

San Diegans responded so well to his role as back-up sports anchor – and propensity to say things like, "Look at Kobe Bryant, as smooth as a sax solo" – that he was quickly elevated to full-time talent. Between his National Football League pension, commercial endorsements, and now television work, Action Jackson had enough money to live in a house in Pacific Beach, drive a flashy car, and fly his parents out for long weekends.

"You made it, son," his father would say, "you done real good."

The ladies noticed too. Sometimes, too many ladies.

That was the case on this New Year's Eve. Teddy had told one girl he'd meet her somewhere by midnight, and earlier he texted another female saying he'd meet up with *her* at some point. It was like Action Jackson was still wearing cleats, only instead of dipping and dodging defenders, he would swerve when a young lady wanted him to commit; he would surge when someone was awed by the fact they'd seen him on TV, either as a player or news figure; he would swoop when a pretty face was clearly attracted to his still-trim body and handsome face.

"I'll settle down someday, Mama," he once told his concerned mother, "but I haven't found the right one yet. I don't wanna choose the wrong girl and end up cheating on her."

It was a convoluted but honest form of morality. In his professional playing days, Jackson had several teammates who married their high school or college sweetheart because those women loved their guys before they were graced with fame and fortune. They could be trusted, was what the players would say. Other athletes got lucrative contracts and then married to essentially start a concubine – while he would score touchdowns, she would raise his kids. Often times both of these types of marriages featured athlete husbands that conveniently ignored their marriage vows. Being young, rich, and famous, with extended amounts of time on the road, led to frequent infidelity.

Teddy could accurately say he'd never cheated on a woman. He might date someone but never exclusively. And no woman could ever boast having his ring on her finger – unless he was flirting and let them wear his Notre Dame class ring or playoff jewelry.

If there was also a trend to Teddy's romances it was this: he was now 35. Considered old for an athlete but still young in the game of life. His ladies du jour were mostly in their 20's. A woman of 27 years was considered not to his liking. Teddy liked 21-year old San Diego State interns, 23-year old Pacific Beach college graduates, and 25-year old club-hopping vixen. They were young, playful, frisky, and entranced by his athletic notoriety and local television fame.

His prowess as a wide receiver often worked on the opposite sex too. A speeding ticket could be dissolved by taking a picture with an admiring cop. There were charitable purposes as well. Teddy would lend his name and face and time to emceeing fundraisers and raise money for non-profit organizations. Action Jackson was always in effect.

That same sort of confidence extended into his new career, as well. With the same type of bravado that led him to crash into other defenders or run routes fearlessly up the middle, with complete disregard for safeties aiming for his head, he led his sports highlights too. Scripts were senseless. Teddy knew enough players and teams and highlights he just called them off the cuff and on the fly. He would jot down occasional phrases and tuck them into his notebook in a desk drawer, but like a playbook, they would be committed to memory and appear at just the right time.

On this night, the final night and newscast of 2015, he glided through his highlights. New Year's Eve references were abundant, like the quarterback who dropped a ball into his receiver's hands like it was the Times Square ball, or the point guard who sealed the game with a shot as sweet as a midnight kiss. Teddy was right, sports did not take a night off on New Year's Eve, and successfully delivering another animated highlight segment fueled his confidence for his after-hours plans.

The newscast was complete by 11:29. Teddy stood and removed his tie by 11:31. He was walking to his car by 11:37.

One of the producers, a portly man named Tom, stopped him in the parking garage on the way out. "Big plans tonight, TJ?"

"Aw, you know, just gonna ring in the New Year with some friends, that's all," Jackson responded with his Taye Diggs smile.

"Now, Teddy, you know I'm your boss AND friend," the middle-aged man said, grasping Jackson's elbow, "so I say this with love, my man. Human Resources is really cracking down on fraternization. Please don't let your friends be young ladies who work here at the station, and please be careful if they post pictures of you drinking, dancing, whatever."

"Fraternization? Do I have to be in a fraternity to do that?" Teddy delivered a playful karate chop as he delivered that punch line.

His boss was not amused. Teddy didn't care.

"Tom, I love you, man, and Happy New Year." With that, Action Jackson flashed a peace sign, got in his candy-red Porsche, and zoomed off.

It was New Year's Eve, nearly midnight, the night was young, and so were Teddy's pending dates. Teddy Jackson was ready for some action.

Beers and Burritos

In San Diego's downtown neighborhood of East Village, Bub's by the Ballpark is a beacon in the night. Located on the corner of Seventh Avenue and J Street, it is a short relay throw from Petco Park. Fancy clubs and expensive eateries don't last in laid-back San Diego. Places like Bub's, with wood flooring and neon lights adorning the entrance, do.

On New Year's Eve, like all other nights, they require no cover charge. Come as you are, in dapper suits to bedrock blue jeans. At 11:45, champagne is handed out in anticipation of the delirious countdown just minutes away. Whereas Bub's normally specializes in tater-tots, on December 31 they are expertise in electricity. Electric cheers, that is.

Teddy Jackson had made it just in time to park his Porsche in a nearby lot, hustle over to Bub's, find his lady friend among the crowd of bustling babes, and plant a wet one when the clock struck twelve. For good measure, he kissed two others and then winked at his date. Initially she was angered but no one could stay mad at Action Jackson, baby.

As the din of the celebrating crowd grew louder, and patrons started looking down at their phones to send and receive congratulatory text messages, Teddy glanced at the bar. He noticed a man with his head down. Was that…?

Teddy edged away from his date and approached the man, who looked very drunk. Where had he seen him before?

"Excuse me," he asked, while approaching the inebriated gentleman, "I know this sounds crazy…and believe me, I'm not hitting on you…but I know you from somewhere."

The lad looked up and said, "Hey! You're Action Jack…"

Teddy cut him off. "The ICON Building…I was at your Christmas party a couple weeks ago! A friend invited me and, well, I ended up leaving with another friend, this hot little…anyways, you were with that blonde girl. The angry one."

"Action Jackson, my name is Fernando," the man said while extending his right hand, "and yes, I was with the blonde girl. She was my….fiancee."

"Oh, cool, man!" Teddy exclaimed.

"WAS my fiancée. She broke up with me. Broke up with me, Teddy!"

Teddy glanced at the half-dozen empty shot glasses in front of this man, Fernando, and quickly ascertained why his words were slurred, his shirt and tie was disheveled, and why he was starting to cry.

"I'm, I'm sorry, man, I really am," Teddy responded. "She's no longer your fiancée?"

With a wail that was a cross between a cry of exasperation and pain, Fernando replied, "Naaaaaaaah, man, nah. She broke up with me. Broke… up…with…."

He then burst into tears and Teddy found himself embracing a man with whom he'd only encountered in a condo hallway a fortnight earlier. The fact he knew Teddy's name and nickname was not unusual, Action

Jackson got stopped all the time. He didn't mind taking a selfie if it got him out of a parking ticket. But this chap was crying into Teddy's $400 blazer. Oh no, this had to stop.

"Alright, there there, now, come on," he intoned in an awkward but comforting manner. Fernando then elevated his head and raised his finger, indicating to the bartender he wanted another beverage.

Teddy interrupted. "Uh, you know what, barkeep? What's his bill? Let me pay it."

Fernando was alert enough to look at him and ask, "What? Why?"

Teddy didn't respond, simply handing the bartender his Black American Express card. "Fernando, you live a few blocks from here, right? Come on, man, we gotta get you home."

"What? Teddy, what are you doing?" It was Teddy's date and she looked as perplexed as she was upset.

"Baby, just stay here, I'll come back," Teddy responded while paying the bill, "but let me help this guy. His fiancée broke up with him and look at him, he's a mess, he can't get home by himself!"

"But my friend's here too," she answered in a whiny voice, "oh, here she is! Her name's…"

"Beatriz!" Fernando had uttered her name, suddenly and loudly.

At the same time, Teddy and his date said, "You know her?"

Fernando nodded. And grinned.

Beatriz was confused. But she nodded too. Indeed, Fernando Guzman had recognized his erstwhile Christmas party guest, Beatriz Feliz. (And Action Jackson too, of course.)

"Water, all I need is a little water," Fernando panted, like a man trudging across the Mojave desert.

The nearby bartender overheard and without having to be asked, poured a glassful of H2O and handed it to Teddy, who handed it to Fernando. The effects of the Fireball shots were mitigated by his gulping of the water.

Beatriz took the opportunity to formally introduce herself. "Hi, I'm Beatriz, I'm a friend of Fernando's. Were you…were you…at his Christmas party?"

"Yes, briefly, I'm Teddy Jackson, or you can call me TJ." Teddy still had a habit from his playing days of introducing himself by his full name.

Women often cooed at that. Beatriz was a football fan but acted like she did not have a clue he was a former gridiron great.

"I was there at the party," Teddy continued, "and I think I saw you briefly. You were there with...your husband?"

"Ex-husband," Bea replied matter-of-factly. She suddenly felt three pairs of eyeballs – Teddy's, Fernando's, and even Teddy's impatient date – intently on her. The music was loud but it was as if silence had engulfed the bar.

"Uh, well, soon to be ex," Beatriz explained. "He recently told me he wants a divorce."

With that she clutched her glass of wine and sarcastically bellowed, "HAPPY New Year!"

"Well hot diggety," Teddy said, "aren't we quite a crew here? He's no longer engaged, you're no longer married, and I'm..."

Teddy's date glared at him. He proceeded anyway: "And I'm still single to mingle!"

And off she goes! Teddy's date stormed away in the direction of the restrooms.

"Oh dear," said Beatriz, "maybe I should follow her and make sure she's alright."

"Aw, leave her be," Teddy waved his hand. "She wasn't my girlfriend anyway. I got 99 problems but that chick ain't one."

"Boom!" exclaimed Fernando, giving Teddy a solid fist bump.

The three laughed.

"She Gone!" Fernando said, while bursting into laughter. He was now less of a sloppy drunk and more of a happy one.

The bartender handed Teddy another water for his inebriated buddy. Fernando grasped it and downed it.

"Well, both of you," Teddy looked at Beatriz and Fernando intently. "What happened?"

Beatriz went first. She knew she'd have to elevate her voice to be heard above the din of the crowd noise and the song *Rump Shaker* overhead. Fernando was dancing to that on his barstool.

"He found somebody else," she half-yelled, "at a new job. Almost ten years, two kids, and lifetime vows down the drain. Maybe I should have seen it coming. Maybe I didn't focus on our relationship as much as I should have. Maybe I'm just an ugly old hag!"

Both gentlemen instantly said *NOOOOOOO!*

"What about you?" Beatriz pointed to Fernando.

"Psssssssssssssht!" he retorted. "Pssssssht! Ain't no story here! I'm a loser. My girl, my FIANCEE, left me because she's not happy. I don't make her happy. I don't…"

Fernando broke down into tears, an ugly and public cry.

"Uh, tell you what," Teddy said, while handing Fernando his – ugh – very expensive hankerchief. "What do you guys say we go talk somewhere a little quieter? Let's blow this taco stand."

The duo looked at him, confused.

"That's racist," Fernando said in a whisper.

Teddy chuckled. "Nah, man, it's an expression. Let's….let's get out of here."

They nodded in agreement.

California Burritos

Lolita's at the Park is not actually at a park. But it's across the street from one, a Major League Baseball park, splendid and sophisticated Petco Park in San Diego. The ballpark was one of the city's gems and Lolita's was directly adjacent to it, on the corner of Park Boulevard and Tenth Avenue.

Named after the owner's wife, it was family-owned but had a distinctive charm that made it feel like it belonged to the East Village. Teddy often came for the California burrito – a burrito crammed with carne asada and french fries – when he reported on Padres games. He often wondered, given their proximity to Petco Park, why the Mexican eatery didn't feature any photos of ballplayers who frequented the place. Athletes from the home *and* road teams would often stop by. They were celebrities. So was he. How come, TJ wondered, my picture's not on a wall, either?

To get from Bub's BY the Ballpark to Lolita's AT the Park, as their names suggest, it took Teddy, Beatriz, and Fernando approximately three blocks, including a winding, twisting turn on Tenth Avenue. But instead of traipsing down the street like Dorothy, the lion, and the scarecrow, Teddy and Beatriz flanked Fernando and held him up as he stumbled forward. The alcohol was still in his system and Teddy just prayed it would not re-emerge in the form of projectile vomiting. They weren't Three Musketeers as much as they were Two and a Half (sober) Men.

Along the way, cars honked their horn and scantily-clad women giggled at Fernando's uneven walking. It was New Year's, although now technically it was New Year's DAY, as the clock had already struck twelve. Everyone was bubbly because they had drank lots of bubbly.

Arriving to Lolita's was like arriving to a therapy session, but with burritos. The troika grabbed a table amid the hammered but hungry revelers, Teddy paid for his friends' meals, and the venting began.

He ordered his typical Cali burrito but Beatriz had the carne asada fries – *just a half-order, please, I'm watching my figure.* Fernando was alert enough to roll his eyes and order the Two-in-One burrito, another interesting Lolita's concoction where they stuffed two rolled tacos into a carne asada burrito for an intriguing mixture of crunchy and soft bites. By now, for all three, Coca-Cola had replaced alcohol. Bea requested Diet Coke, though, you know, 'cause of her figure.

For a change, though, Teddy didn't do much talking. He didn't show much Action. He listened, serving as dimestore psychologist and erstwhile marriage counselor.

Fernando began: "I'm just stunned, man. I gave her everything she wanted. I'd surprise her with flowers. I'd stick little love letters in her suitcase when she traveled. I texted her, like, every hour to see how her day was going. I proposed to her at Disneyland. How romantic is THAT? At Disneyland! I paid for every meal and showered her with affection. And she left me. She left me, man."

Bea then jumped in: "Maybe you showed her TOO much affection? Maybe she wasn't surprised anymore? Heck, I'm not one to talk. At least you focused on your relationship. I was so busy getting the kids to soccer games, and ballet practice, and my parents to doctors' appointments, maybe I didn't focus ENOUGH on the relationship. But isn't that what a good wife does? Caters to her family needs? And I have my career and my responsibilities, I'm a proud and successful Latina. How could he just… dump…me?"

"They didn't appreciate us, Bea," said a forlorn Fernando. "We gave them everything and they didn't appreciate us!"

"Like, are you Beyonce and we're Destiny's Child?" Bea asked rhetorically. "Are you all that, to leave your fiancée and spouse? Please. Our two knuckleheads lost the best thing to ever happen to them, Freddie."

Teddy laughed and high-fived them both.

Fernando then asked, "What do I do now, TJ? I'm…I'm all alone."

Teddy didn't really know how to respond to that. Except to blurt out, "You're not alone. You've got me. I mean, I know I barely know you two. But BOTH of you. You got ME. You got US."

Chapter 4

Jenn with Two N's

Jennifer Holtz

It was winter 2016.

Why is the cost of living so high in San Diego? One reason is because winter should really be signified with quotes around the word.

"Winter."

It certainly is different than the other three seasons, in that it is noticeably cooler and it rains with more frequency. But there are also days of brilliant blue skies and shimmering sunshine. While much of the United States deals with snow, ice, hail, sleet, and freezing rain, San Diego has…"winter."

As they stepped into Lolita's taco shop on New Year's Eve, Jennifer Holtz was trying to explain this to her date, Jack 'Murph' Murphy.

"I know it costs a lot to live here," Jenn was saying as they neared the entrance, "and you're a native, and I came from Wisconsin, so it's more expensive to me no matter what, whereas you've *seen* the cost of living rise. But look at where we live!"

Murph rolled his eyes and prepared to hold the door open for Jenn. They were in that stage where in the last few weeks they had hung out more, enough to where he asked her to be his New Year's Eve date, and gave her the requisite kiss at midnight, but not yet formally boyfriend and girlfriend. Yet it was early enough in their budding romance where holding doors open was a sweet, unexpected gesture.

She cooed, "Awwww, thank you!"

Jenn had several fairly predictable patterns. If someone sent her an e-mail or text message and spelled her first name 'Jen', she would remind them: It's Jenn. With two n's. She would then add a smiley-face emoticon to emphasize a tone of pleasantness and benevolence.

That was also very characteristically Jenn. Constantly upbeat. Eternally optimistic. Exceedingly kind. Perpetually seeing the good.

Thus far in their dating experience, it was a good balance. Jenn was supremely sweet and Jack was a little rougher around the edges – pragmatic at worst and realistic at best.

As she entered the eatery, BOOM! An obviously tipsy woman holding a fountain drink barreled right into her. The drink splattered all over Jenn's pristine, white dress. Right in her stomach area now would be a big, dark stain.

This woman was flanked by two men, one was Hispanic and also inebriated and a tall black man, who seemed more sedate.

Yet, it was Jenn who apologized. Murph hated that.

"Oh my gash!" she exclaimed in her Wauwatosa, Wisconsin brogue. "I'm so sorry. Are you ok?"

The drunk duo laughed fervently. Their friend, clearly a chaperone, said, "She's fine. I'm sorry she ran into you."

"Oh that's fine, I'm fine," Jenn responded, although the ice cubes suddenly left a very cold feeling on her mid-section.

"I'm sorry, I'm so sorry," said the collision initiator.

"You SHOULD be, Beatriz, geez," said her other giggly male friend in half-feigned indignation.

Murph and the apologetic black gentleman both stooped down to clean up the spilled soda, ice cubes, and pride. That was when Murph got a good look at him and said, "Hey, I've seen you on TV! Are you...?"

His fellow clean-up partner smiled and said, "I'm Teddy Jackson. Some people call me Action. You can call me TJ."

"Oh yeah! I followed you when you were a Charger and I watch you on the news all the time. Real honor to meetcha'," Murph gushed while shaking TJ's hand.

Jenn was in disbelief. She had never seen her normally cynical significant other so enthralled to meet someone. Even more startling was when he asked this Jackson character to take a selfie with him.

Teddy obliged and Jack was still giddy: "You're Jackson and my first name's Jack. If we combined our names, it'd be, like, Jack Jackson! Crazy, right?"

The whole group – Fernando, Beatriz, and Jenn – stared at them.

Murph then asked, "So whaddya' think? Are the Chargers moving to Los Angeles?"

Teddy responded as if someone punched him in his stomach, despite his many abdomen muscles. "*Uuuuuf!* That's a tough question to answer, my man, I don't even wanna THINK of that possibility."

"Me neither, bro!" Murph responded emphatically.

The Chargers leaving San Diego, their home since 1961, was a real possibility as 2016 dawned. Since 2000, their team ownership had asked the City of San Diego for funding for a new stadium. Qualcomm Stadium, their home, was old and dilapidated, every year more and more so. But San Diego was not in positive financial shape at the turn of the New Millenium. A series of political missteps had fiscally drained city coffers, to where the city was known as "Enron by the Sea" – a nod to the Houston energy corporation who had cooked their numbers until finally the company crumbled under corruption and greed.

San Diego, America's Finest City, didn't have one corporation emblematic of its financial mess, but found itself embroiled in political and economic turmoil. In short, it was not a good time for Dean Spanos and his family to come seeking tax subsidies.

But still they tried. And eventually both the national and local economies improved, though the 2008 housing and banking markets plummeted early that fall. By then the Chargers were frustrated and their demeanor toward the city turned caustic. One thing about the National Football League, they expected cities to pony up for new stadiums and dangled Super Bowls as carrots for 'yes' votes on tax increases and public subsidies.

For the next seven years, as elected officials locally came in and out of office, promises were uttered to work with the Chargers on developing a proposal for a new stadium. San Diego is a different kind of town, though. As Jenn noted to Jack, it had a high cost of living; ostensibly a "sunshine tax." And looking at soaring housing costs and an escalating homeless problem, residents were not eager to raise their taxes to fund a stadium. Rightly or wrongly, it also correlated with the team having superb seasons but getting bounced from the playoffs in heart-crushing fashion.

In 2004, their first postseason appearance in nearly a decade, placekicker Nate Kaeding missed a chip-shot field-goal attempt in overtime at home versus the New York Jets in the first round. The Chargers were eliminated. In 2006, a 14-2 Chargers squad hosted the New England Patriots and fell apart in spectacular fashion, amid turnovers and mental errors like safety Marlon McCree getting stripped of a would-be game-winning interception. Even the head coach who resurrected them from mediocrity, Marty Schottenheimer, incurred an unsportsmanlike penalty at one point for leaving the sidelines to woof at the referees. Shortly after the disastrous loss, Schottenheimer was fired. The next two head coaches hired to replace him would eventually be canned too.

In 2007, the "Bolts" – a nickname based on their thunderbolt insignia – made it all the way to the American Football Conference championship game. Needing one more win to reach the Super Bowl, heights only attained in 1995, a slew of injuries to their best players derailed them and the Chargers lost a competitive game at frigid New England. 2008 brought a quick second-round exit in Pittsburgh and 2009 ushered in another heartbreaking home loss to the Jets amid two more Kaeding missed field goals in a close loss. Kaeding was jettisoned and so, a year later, was head coach Norv Turner. Another organizational comeback arose when the club made it to the postseason tournament in 2013. But the departure was in the second round and fans, by then, were weary.

Any hopes for a new stadium funded by taxpayers seemed as gone as the team's Super Bowl hopes. As contract clauses were triggered for the team to explore a move – Los Angeles was a likely destination – an air of finality cloaked the city like morning clouds near the coastline.

"It's going to be quite a year," Teddy said while helping clean up the final remnants of Beatriz colliding into Jen. "If the Chargers leave and Trump becomes President…"

Ah, yes, Donald John Trump. Another sore or favorite, depending on his mood, of Teddy's was politics. His producers, just as they had warned him to not date younger staff members, also reprimanded him for a couple political opinions he had divulged on the air. Nothing too controversial or offensive, but the message was clear: we can't alienate half of our audience; please keep your political views to yourself. His news colleagues would then egg him on, sometimes minutes before a telecast, by telling him the latest soundbites from millionaire-turned-Republican-nominee Donald Trump. They dubbed Teddy "Reaction Jackson" because he'd get so steamed.

His new friends, Fernando and Beatriz, didn't know this about him. Neither did his sudden but ardent admirer, Jack Murphy. Teddy used to be good, as an athlete, with the press because he was loquacious. The reporters loved coming to him for an entertaining quote, even after a mundane day of practice. Teddy knew how to liven things up. And he was great at his current profession as a sports analyst because he could go on television or even guest-spot on radio and talk about any athletic subject. Football, baseball, basketball, soccer, and more – if it bounced, he watched it. One could say the same about him and the ladies too.

But politics was forbidden. They were too divisive and everyone – from his bosses to his agent to his Mama back in South Bend, Indiana – warned him: *Don't talk about politics, Teddy. It doesn't matter which side you're on, somebody is bound to get mad. And they may turn you off their television or radio dial.*

In his previous profession, Teddy was adjudged on receiving yards and touchdowns. As a broadcaster, he was evaluated by how many viewers he had and, in this day and age of social media presence, the metrics applied were called "engagement." How many fans watched him on the news and shared his catch-phrases or witticisms on their Facebook or Twitter feeds?

His supporters were concerned that his clear disdain for Donald Trump would turn him off to San Diegans who liked the mop-haired candidate or simply wanted to tune out political discussions and focus solely on teams and how many points they scored.

Teddy didn't care. He had opinions and an audience and he wanted his viewpoint to reach his followers.

"It'll be a travesty, Murph. Can I call you Murph?"

"Sure, most people call me tha-"

Teddy cut him off. "Murph, imagine if a REALITY TELEVISION STAR becomes our next United States President. This man has no experience in governance. He has no leadership traits. His businesses have gone bankrupt. He's already said things to offend people, especially people of color. I tell you, he's certainly no Barack Obama."

Knowing that her aspiring beau and sudden soda-stain cleaner was no fan of the current President, Jenn jumped in. She also didn't care much for political discourse, knowing it usually devolves into divisive debate, and didn't want Jack's elation of meeting Action Jackson to turn into a feisty fight.

"Uhhhh, we don't wanna keep you guys. Sweetie, are you sure you're ok?" Jenn had turned to Beatriz, who nodded that she was fine.

Of course she's fine, SHE rammed into you, Murph thought to himself.

"Tell you what, here's my business card," said Teddy, while pulling his card out of his wallet. "Send me an e-mail and we should all have dinner sometime in the East Village."

Murph held the card like it was a trading card from childhood, the collectibles that were adorned with football and baseball player names, photographs, and a mountain of statistics. He used to have boxes of those and couldn't understand why his younger siblings and nephews now treated them like they were old cassette tapes. Trading cards had become obsolete but business cards were seemingly always in play.

"Dinner with Action Jackson?" Murph gushed, "Sign me up!"

"Uh, but only on one condition," said Teddy.

"What's that?" Murph inquired.

"That you bring your girl and I bring my friends," Teddy replied, pointing to Fernando and Beatriz. "They're my, they're my, uh, they're my Wolfpack."

Everyone – Jack, Jenn, Fernando, Bea – looked at Teddy like he had a third eye on his forehead. Wolfpack? What did he mean by that?

"Sure," Murph responded, "your Wolfpack. That's what's up."

Dark Clouds

Jennifer Holtz never had a shortage of things to do. Her professional life in public relations were full of press releases, media pitches, and promotional events, a frenzied pace of writing and phone calls. On top of that, seemingly every weekend was booked with a 5K or half-marathon to raise funds for AIDS awareness, cancer treatments, or mental illness. She bought Girl Scout cookies and then donated them to people were homeless. She practiced yoga as a way to both get physical exercise and cleanse herself of any overly stressful thoughts. And Jenn – with two n's, mind you – loved inspirational quotes, dotting her office cubicle with sayings from Maya Angelou to Tony Robbins to Mother Theresa.

She was the eternal optimist, something that the rather jaded Jack Murphy found endearing. They had met via an online dating service. Jenn found Murph to be ruggedly handsome and Murph, besides noticing that she was cute and freckled, appreciated her passion for causes. All *he* really felt passionate about was Taco Tuesday.

There was one dark cloud, however, in Jenn's perpetually blue sky. She was very close with her mom, Lucy. And Lucy was very sick.

Jenn first noticed something was amiss during the weekly mother-daughter brunches they shared. She was close to her father too but this was "girl time", an opportunity to chit-chat and indulge in some gossip or review the most recent episode of *The Bachelorette*. On this sunny morning, however, Lucy seemed low on energy, which was very unlike her.

"I think I'm just tired," Lucy said, waving her hand as she grabbed a scone at Balboa Park, "I just need a good rest."

"Mom, you're walking kind of strange," Jenn noted, "let's get you a check-up. I'm sure it'll be fine."

It wasn't fine. Lucy Holtz was diagnosed with Multiple Sclerosis, a debilitating condition that would impact her ability to walk, talk, and eventually see. Jenn was rocked.

Would she lose her mother? What would her mom, who was her best friend, have to endure? Jenn was extremely concerned.

The only way to not be preoccupied with worry was to stay busy. Jenn could ace that easily.

Her firm's top client, a mobile technology client, was unveiling a new product line that winter. So a whole publicity package had to be created. There were a couple 5K races coming up that encouraged teams to enroll so she had to muster support for that. Things were going well with Murph and not to look too far ahead, but Valentine's Day was only a month away.

Murph, sweet ol' Murph. He was so thrilled to meet Action Jackson, Jenn took the initiative of e-mailing the former athlete and current sportscaster. She proposed two dates for dinner when she knew her and her man – boyfriend? Significant other? That was still up in the air – were free and wanted to check on the availability of Teddy and his friends.

She fired off the e-mail and was surprised to get a response less than 15 minutes later. Teddy accepted a Thursday night option.

Jenn wrote back, with a smiley face: COOL BEANS.

It was set. Jenn and Murph were having dinner with the Wolfpack.

Text Wars

A new routine had been established. Although Fernando and Beatriz were still grieving the loss of their relationships – and actually *because* Fernando and Beatriz were still grieving the loss of their relationships – Fernando made a new rule. Monday nights were reserved for him to host Bea and Teddy to his now-emptier condo for dinner and television. With Monday Night Football now over, there was a void. Freddy also noticed another void: not having a live-in lover meant weekends were especially tough. He and Katie had a set routine. Dinner as "date night" on Friday evenings, a movie on Saturday, and on Sunday they went to church and had a good jog down by the waterfront Embarcadero. Katie once said something about needing to break the monotony but Fernando said, "There's no monotony here. Just a good, reliable schedule for us. I love it."

Now with no one to share popcorn with at the theaters and tell stories to while jogging at the harbor, weekends were sad. They felt unfulfilled.

Bea agreed.

Teddy saw that Beatriz said yes to Fernando's offer of Monday night dinners, viewings of *The Bachelorette*, and wine and lively discussions, so he agreed to attend too.

Oh Teddy was definitely noticing Beatriz Feliz.

She was still in her prime, with long, brown cascading hair, supple lips, and a ravishing olive-oil complexion, ample bosom, and toned legs that belied her hours upon hours at her gymnasium's Stair Master. Although she had given birth twice, she worked hard to get back to an hourglass shape. Beatriz worked hard at everything, from her job, to taking care of her kids, to ensuring a good life for her parents, to working out – if she knew she couldn't do it after work, she'd wake up an hour early to squeeze in her exercise -, to volunteering for the campaign of Presidential candidate Hillary Clinton. Action Jackson liked all that.

Problem was, Fernando noticed it too.

He loved Beatriz's sultry Spanish words and could offer replies. He appreciated that Bea had old-school family values but was a modern, well-educated Latina with feminist sensibilities. He missed Katie, to be sure, but knew it was time for him to move on. If Katie McDonald wasn't walking through that condominium door anytime soon, he had to be open to noticing other women. That pained him but every time he saw Bea his heartache felt a little more soothed.

Teddy versus Freddy. The adoration of Bea was too subtle, too introverted, for the two men to be called friendly rivals. Besides, they generally had grown to like and respect each other as buddies, compadres, and, as Teddy termed it, "road dogs". (Fernando winced at this.)

But like a simmering volcano, the two men's emotions simmered.

Once she put her kids to bed, Beatriz had a routine. Pour a glass of wine, sit on the couch, and catch up with her phone – meaning, respond to text messages, e-mails, and social media posts. As the New Year began to unfold, however, she noticed a new trend emerging. Her phone started buzzing with texts, independently, from Teddy and Fernando.

Fernando's would typically say:

> *Y do u park on a driveway & drive on a parkway?*
> *OMG – tamale overload over here*
> *Mexican word of the day: cheese. Example: leave her alone, cheese mine!*

Bea would giggle at these. She and Fernando certainly had a shared cultural bond, one which he knew how to stoke and do the most important thing every man strives to do with women: make them laugh. But Fernando was so fresh off being dumped by Katie. Was he trying to allure Beatriz? Or were they just Freddy and Bea, newfound buds? She was still deciphering this and analyzing it, knowing that tended to be the biggest challenge most women had: overanalyzing things.

Teddy, meanwhile, would send his own series of texts:

> *Sup girl, how was your day?*
> *Why did Beyonce marry Jay-Z? Didn't she know that baby would look like a UFO?*
> *Trump CANNOT be president! What an incompetent, racist, orange-faced joke!!!!*

He was big on emojis too, dotting each phrase with a picture. Whereas Fernando would incorporate lots of hashtags – such as #FirstWorldProblems when a Starbucks barista called him "Armando" – Teddy would literally type out "Hashtag". As in: Hashtag Cray Cray. She giggled at his texts too, but mainly because he was a bit older and grappling with cellular technology and social media, and also because Teddy was a fairly obvious flirt. But was he flirting with her because he was developing a crush, or because TJ, well, was just being TJ? Flirting came as naturally to him as people reflexively saying, "Hi" whenever one says, "How you doin'?" That's what Bea had to figure out.

For certain, given *her* unexpected, devastating, heart-wrenching – and it appeared, soon to be messy – divorce once proceedings would officially be under way, dating was the LAST thing on her mind right now. She knew she was vulnerable and who knows, maybe a guy with intentions of sleeping with her could catch her on a night of too many cocktails. But Beatriz had a strong moral code too, passed down by her parents, who she truly didn't want to disappoint, and getting intimate with a man was not what she desired while she was still married. Even when the divorce would officially be finalized, she imagined, it would take some time to want to date and even more time to crawl into bed with someone.

Did TJ or Freddy want to do the nasty with her? Or did one or both honestly like her? 'Cause she LIKED them – but as friends only. For all of the reasons outlined, maybe she should just assign them into the Friend Zone. That's a zone where lust and love go to disappear. But what if she eventually liked one?

If she told one she had to decline an invitation in order to be with the other, the text responses were typically:

No Bueno. Maybe next time.
Or
Fur real? That's just too dang bad.

Beatriz LOVED these guys though. They were earnestly helping her get through the trauma and deep-seeded disappointment of her husband leaving her for another woman.

Couldn't everyone just get along and be homies?

Dinner: A Comedy of Debates

Though it was a little too upscale for her budget, Jenn agreed to Teddy's suggestion that their group dinner be held at Water Grill, just a block from Bub's. The seafood and steak establishment had earned the highest stars on Yelp and given that befriending Action Jackson had brought out Murph's inner fan – and child – she figured the high cost was worthwhile.

She called ahead and made reservations for the group under her name, telling the hostess, "Please save it under Jenn. With two n's."

It was like Christmas or New Year's or Major League Baseball Opening Day for Murph. He circled it on his calendar and counted down the days.

When the day and dinner hour arrived, the group assembled in the lobby to avoid the evening chill. It was drizzling, which meant these San Diegans were wearing their thickest boots and most plush scarves. Teddy was, per his habit, late. The hostess seated them anyway and brought fresh bread and waters until TJ arrived.

When he did, remembering their January 1 introductions, he said, "Hey there, Jack."

"Aw please, call me Murph," said Jenn's man.

"Alright then, Murph," replied Teddy, and with his eyes shifting to Jenn, so did his voice. "And hello, Jennifer."

It was a deeper octave and he grabbed Jenn's hand to kiss the back of it.

"Oh, Teddy, you're such a flirt," she said coyly.

Then he noticed Beatriz there and kissed her hand too. She rolled her eyes.

As the group sat down, there was the customary awkwardness and stiff conversation. Fernando offered, "Can you believe this crazy weather?"

Everyone nodded and Jenn thought to herself: *Crazy Californians, always freaked out by a little rain.* But she didn't verbalize it for fear of anyone getting offended.

Teddy asked, for anyone to answer, "So who do you guys like in the Super Bowl?"

Bea responded quickly, "If my Cowboys aren't playin', then I don't care."

Murph retorted, "The Cowboys? Come on now. They're never getting into another Super Bowl. Tony Romo is the biggest choker for a quarterback ever."

Bea snapped, "Please, you're a Chargers fan, that whole team chokes. They'll be in L.A. soon anyway."

The whole group groaned. Teddy jokingly feigned emotional pain: "Too soon, Beatriz, too soon."

Everyone chuckled and Jenn said, "Well I hear the Broncos are pretty good, but I just watch for the commercials and halftime performer. This year it's Coldplay, Beyonce, AND Bruno Mars."

"Oh those are the WORST," Murph opined.

"What are you talking about? Those are the BEST," Teddy answered.

"I know Beyonce's the best, and I can care less about her singing, am I right?" Fernando punctuated that statement with a high five to Teddy. It was somewhat rare to see high fives anymore. Most people, no matter the occasion, had evolved toward fist bumps. Really, those were considered more masculine whereas high fives were now more customary for ladies. Still, the two men at the table who cared the most about their manliness engaged in a loud, flesh-slapping high five.

"You guys are crazy," Jenn ducked in, "Coldplay will blow her away."

"What?!" Bea was fired up. "Beyonce has big hips and Coldplay is super-boring. Bruno Mars will kill it."

"Was that a pun?" Teddy intoned, "SUPER boring?"

The group laughed but Bea re-asserted herself. "No, I'm serious as a heart attack. Bruno Mars can sing, dance, and he's sexy. He's the whole package."

"I BET you'd like to see his package," said Murph. He hardly knew Beatriz at all but felt emboldened to make that joke. He could tell she was a big girl, capable of adult-content jokes.

Jenn nearly spit up her wine but laughed too. Hitting him across the chest, she playfully admonished him – *Murph!*

"Well no matter how those three do," Teddy chimed in, "they will never top the best halftime performance of all time."

The table was silent. Everyone looked at Action Jackson inquisitively.

He buttered a biscuit and then stated, almost triumphantly: "Michael. Jackson."

AWWWW, WHAAAAAAT! NO WAY! PLEASE! The reaction was as unanimous as it was widespread and loud.

"What? Michael rules," Teddy replied, looking stunned.

"Hey, I got nothin' but love for Michael, but better than Prince?" asked Murph.

"Better than his sister Janet and Justin Timberlake and their 'wardrobe malfunction'?" inquired Fernando, putting the last two words into air quotes.

"Better than Nelly and N'SYNC?" piped in Jenn.

AHHHHHHHHHHHHHHHHHHH! With that, a flood of napkins, razzes, and laughter were all hurled Jennifer's way.

When the groans and moans died down, Murph leaned back into his chair and said, "I have a question. How did you guys all become friends?"

His attention had shifted from being an ardent fan of Action Jackson to noticing the obvious chemistry within the group.

A nervous laughter permeated the environment. Initially, no one said anything.

After a few awkward seconds of fork-shuffling and glasses clinking, Fernando spoke up: "Well, I knew Teddy and Bea from here in the East Village. But we really didn't closely know each other until we had heartbreak."

"Heartbreak?" Murph and Jenn asked in unison.

"'Heartbreak' is the name of New Edition's best-selling album ever," Teddy said, citing his favorite rhythm and blues group of all-time. No one knew what he was talking about.

Fernando continued: "We've been bonded by heartbreak. My fiancée left me and Beatriz's husband left her. And Teddy here, he hasn't really experienced that type of heartbreak, but he kind of helps us hold things together."

"I'll be heartbroken if Trump wins the election, I'll tell you that much," Teddy interjected with a sassy head shake.

Murph rolled his eyes and said, "I like Trump."

Teddy pretended not to hear him and continued on: "Actually, I was pretty devastated when my football career ended. It was all I knew. So I think having experienced that helps me in dealing with the heartache being felt by these two."

"So you're, like, the leader of the crew?" Jenn surmised.

"We're a Wolfpack," Teddy said with a smile, "but actually, did you know a Wolfpack leader is not in the front?"

Everyone was transfixed. Teddy continued: "In packs of wolves, you would think the alpha dog would be out in front, right? But the lead wolf actually hangs back and stays BEHIND the pack. He makes sure the other wolves are safe first. Now I'm not sayin' I'm the lead wolf here. But I'm a little older than these two. I moved away from my family to start my pro career and eventually, like every athlete, I lost that career. So I've experienced some things. And I'm gonna help these two get through it. Wolfpack hooooowl!"

With that, Fernando and Beatriz raised their glasses of wine, so Murph and Katie did too. Teddy initiated a toast: "To the Wolfpack!"

The group followed suit: *To the Wolfpack!*

Then Murph added, "'N'SYNC still sucks."

Chapter 5

Springing Forward

Teddy Jackson hated spring training. Actually the process of spring training – players preparing for the Major League Baseball season and fans having much closer access to pictures and autographs – weren't things he minded. And he certainly didn't mind the leisurely pace and spring break-like schedule, which afforded him many nights at the Salty Senorita cantina. There he could socialize with many young ladies who descended upon Peoria, Arizona, and other spring training locales in the desert, and many players did too.

What he disliked were the games themselves. Long, tedious baseball exhibitions where starters played scant innings and minor leaguers dotted rosters in hopes of making the Opening Day cut, while wearing jersey numbers more suitable for football linemen. 78, 92, and 96 were among the digits on jerseys that even the most optimistic fan knew would not be in major league ballparks that summer.

But because Teddy was a sports anchor for San Diego's television sports affiliate, he was assigned to spend two complete weeks in the strip-mall and franchise restaurant capital of the world – or so it seemed to Teddy – of Peoria. That meant a five-hour drive from pristine San Diego to dusty Arizona, with only a stop in between at the McDonald's in Yuma. The Padres held their spring training camps there from 1969-1995 before being lured away, closer to Phoenix, by the new stadium and facility built by the City of Peoria. The stadium and training fields were shared with the

Seattle Mariners, a common practice in Major League Baseball, and Teddy didn't doubt their dazzling design.

However, when your nickname is Action, that's what you crave, and spring training exhibition games seldom provided that. They were long and monotonous and most of the time the starters were gone by mid-game and already on the front nine of Arizona's many splendid golf courses. To even get an interview, whether it be with cagey veterans or hotshot rookies, Teddy had to arrive to the practice fields by 7 a.m., an hour to which he was very unaccustomed. He was Action Jackson, a star. Up by 6 to go conduct taped interviews? *This is nonsense*, he told his producers, *shhhhooot*.

The games, though, were the worst part. Sitting in a cramped press box, with the desert heat a-blazing, watching players he knew he wouldn't see past March 31. Even the veterans treated spring ball quite differently. Pitchers experimented with different throwing angles and deliveries and didn't care if they gave up home runs. They were just trying to loosen up their arms, plus they could always hide behind the excuse that the ball flies in the arid Arizona air. Hitters, too, approached their at-bats differently, swinging aggressively, even wildly, and just trying to establish a rhythm – and get the game over with. Final scores didn't matter. The only thing everyone did in unison was get tan.

So Teddy sat in his assigned seat in the press box and did what his bosses asked him to do more of: Tweet. Social media numbers meant as much to them as television ratings and provided that coveted word: engagement. Between his venerated playing days, sculpted jaw, broad shoulders, and unfiltered opinions on current sports topics, Teddy had great potential. Every post on Twitter, Facebook, and Instagram had thousands of followers and scores of comments.

Thus Teddy watched. And reacted. And posted.

In spring training, promising rookies were termed by him "young bucks." He would comment on their hair do's, from "beautiful locks" to "fresh fades." He even made compliments, like "Sanchez's arm is as strong as Whitney Houston's vocal chords." And if a player didn't run out a ground ball to first? "Arrest that man! He's stealing from his employer!"

But sometimes, spring training games ran long. And there wasn't a lot of action that inspired commentary. It was then that Teddy's mind would wander. So would his fingers, specifically toward live links on his laptop. As much as he loved and consumed athletics, Teddy Jackson was an educated man. He immersed himself in music, cinema, and politics. His opinions were strong on many topics, none more so than politics.

It was a gorgeous afternoon in the aptly-named Valley of the Sun, where the late February clouds lifted just past noon. Just in time for a spring training game featuring way too many rookies and not enough base hits. Teddy shot his daily pre-game feature of an established or promising young player and then retreated to his seat in the press box. He knew he should be thankful to have this dream job, a gig that millions would give their left arm for, but frankly he was bored. The game was boring. The Tweets he sent out were boring. All of this was boring.

So he started clicking on other web sites from news sources. CNN. MSNBC. Fox Nows. And he couldn't believe what he was reading. Donald Trump was running in the Presidential primaries for the Republican party. Running steadfastly. And running his mouth.

When Teddy started reading that Trump was advocating for a wall alongside the United States-Mexico border, ostensibly to keep out "murderers, rapists, and thieves," he was livid. He Tweeted: HOW DARE MR. TRUMP TALK ABOUT MY MEXICAN BROTHERS AND SISTERS LIKE THAT? And when he learned Trump's debate methodology was to criticize and ridicule other candidates, it didn't sit well with Teddy. His post: #TRUMP IS A CHILDISH, INCOMPETENT CLOWN WHO KNOWS HOW TO INSULT, BUT NOT RUN A COUNTRY. Sometimes it was hard to contain his rage within 140 characters. Though they didn't say anything via e-mails or text messages, Teddy knew his bosses back home were squirming.

Finally after four long hours of mind-numbing baseball – who won? Who cares? – Teddy started packing up his laptop. A young, aspiring television reporter from Phoenix approached him.

"Mr. Jackson, my name's Vanessa, I work here locally for KSUN," she said while extending her hand. Vanessa had straight, long, feathery hair and curves like the mountains between San Diego and the Imperial Valley.

"Please, my father's not here. Don't call me Mr. Jackson. Call me Teddy, or TJ."

"Teddy, awwww, like a teddy bear," Vanessa giggled. "Anyways, a bunch of us from the station are joining some Padres and Mariners front-office peeps for happy hour at the Salty Señorita. Wanna join us?"

Teddy only needed two seconds to think it through. A chance to network with people within sports media AND front office colleagues, including the comely young sports reporter before him? What else was he going to do in Peoria that night? Count how many Circle K convenience stores there were?

Jackson was ready for some Action.

"Sounds divine," he said, "I'll be there."

At the Salty Señorita, a good time is just a short walk away. Located behind centerfield of the Padres and Mariners shared spring training stadium, one just had to traverse the back parking lot and dodge cars and even golf carts – an Arizona staple - leaving the stadium. And paradise, in the form of nacho chips and thirsty baseball fans, was within reach.

Teddy told himself he'd spend an hour or two there. But happy hour turned into happy *hours*. Two turned into three, and then four, hours. Afternoon turned into dusk. Dusk turned into nightfall, although the interior of the saloon was dark the entire time anyway. Classic party songs spilled out from the jukebox: *Come On Eileen; Whoop There It Is; Poison.* Good times and laughter flowed like the margaritas and Mexican beer. Tequila shots came too, though Teddy didn't remember ordering any of those.

"Hey, that *Poison* song was by Bell Biv DeVoe. They used to be part of New Edition," he said in a slurred voice. No one knew what he was talking about.

Eventually Vanessa and her crew, which included a flock of buxom beauties, mentioned they were going to another bar across town in Scottsdale. "You should come," she urged him.

Having slowed down the last hour to water and carne asada tacos, Teddy smiled and said, "Why not? I'm still young and hip and fun."

Vanessa chuckled, "You're crazy."

Teddy responded, "Crazy about YOU. Ha! My car's across the street at La Quinta Inn. Text me the address and I'll drive and meet you there."

Vanessa hesitated. "Are you sure you're ok to drive? Why don't you share an Uber with us?"

Teddy's face became contorted. "Girl! *Psssht!* I've HOSTED more happy hours than you've ever attended. I'm fine, I'm fine!"

He waved her away and grabbed his keys and cell phone, so Vanessa backed away.

As he'd planned, Teddy walked, in a shuffled type of gait, across the street and down the block to his spring training residence, La Quinta Inn. He specifically asked his bosses for a condo while he was in Peoria. They gave him a hotel room. *They don't respect me*, he thought to himself on this chilly, starry Arizona night.

He climbed into his sports car. He got the address and plugged it into his GPS. He rolled down the windows and cranked up his music, a loud selection from Nelly – young enough that millennials respected it, but old enough that Teddy actually liked it, in comparison to today's crappy and unimaginative hip-hop.

Things looked a little blurry and the skies were certainly dark. Teddy found himself swerving but it was ok, he was fine. He was in control. He was Action Jackson.

Oh man, he was starting to get sleepy too. He rolled down the window a little more.

That's when he heard it. And saw them.

Red lights flashing. And whirring, a screaming sound.

They were sirens. Red lights, blue lights, ominous lights. They were right behind him.

Right behind him.

Teddy looked in his rear view mirror. He knew it instantly.

He was getting pulled over.

The next morning Teddy's head pounded like a worker on one of Peoria's many construction sites was drilling directly into his head. Making matters worse, as he peered out from the sheets of his bed, and squinted into the rising sun beyond his window, was adjacent to his hotel room *was* a construction site *with* a worker drilling into the ground!

He was still drowsy from only obtaining about three hours of sleep. The whole night, from the third tequila shot on, was a blur. He remembers drinking some more, getting into his sports car, driving a bit, and then hearing the sirens. They wailed still in his head.

Still tasting the tequila every time he burped, Teddy recalled walking in a not-so-straight-line for a rather unfriendly officer, and failing at other aspects of a sobriety test. That led to handcuffs, which led to a ride in the police car to their station, which led to mug shots. From the police car to the mug shots, so many flashing lights.

As the haze of the morning, both in the skies and in his awakening, began to lift, Teddy reached for his nightstand. He grabbed his cell phone, which was next to the receipt stating he had been released from jail by posting his own bail. Somehow, probably out of rote habit, he remembered to plug his phone into its charger.

He sat up and uttered, *Oh man!*

Then, after he turned the phone on, it exploded with vibrations. Again, but louder, *oh man!*

Notifications galore. He did not know which came first, the Tweets or the texts or the voicemails, but they all essentially said the same thing: SPORTSCASTER AND FORMER PRO FOOTBALL PLAYER ARRESTED FOR DUI.

His heart sank. He scrolled through the missed calls and three jumped out at him in alarming fashion:

> *Missed Call – Mama*
> *Missed Call – Fernando Guzman*
> *Missed Call - Work*

A feeling of shame coursed through his veins. Unlike his time on the gridiron, there was nowhere to run and nowhere to hide.

Figuring the conversations with Mama and Freddy might be emotional and long-winded, replete with questions, he decided to call his boss first. It felt ominous but also like the right thing to do.

There was no chit-chit, which was their custom. Teddy right away said, "Yes, yes, I'm ok. And I am so, so sorry."

The voice at the other end of the line wasn't his producer or floor director. It was his general manager, Gordon Mayhew.

"Look, Gordo," Teddy began, hoping the occasional nickname he gave Gordon would alleviate some tension. It did not.

"Teddy, I'm glad to hear you're ok, but you know what we have to do," said Gordon, "and this really pains me. But my hands are tied. We told you to stop making political posts. We told you to stop fraternizing with young ladies, especially within our company. But this is the most egregious mistake of all. Teddy, you've been charged with Driving Under the Influence. We have zero tolerance for that, it sends a bad message to our viewers, especially kids. Teddy...please come back to San Diego immediately...and gather your belongings. You're fired."

The last two words hit Teddy like a ton of bricks. He felt physically weakened. Tears suddenly streamed down his cheeks.

His face felt hot. He barely noticed the click on the other end of the line. Gordon hanging up was a hurtful yet barely noticed exclamation mark.

Teddy lost his job.

Action Jackson was no more.

The construction worker drilled on.

Liz Wong

"Pour me another one, Liz," said the sandy-haired blonde man. His Hawaiian shirt was unbuttoned down to his naval and his shorts were much higher than what most men wore these days. His sandals were barely clinging to his barstool at a rustic hole-in-the-wall in Pacific Beach.

"I think you've had enough, sir," she replied. He had seen her nametag but she didn't bother to ask his name. In her mind she had already dubbed him HULK BRADSHAW as his blonde hair and bushy mustache reminded her of a cross between famed wrestler Hulk Hogan and legendary quarterback and television personality Terry Bradshaw. She didn't really watch much football but Kris liked it.

"I said pour me another one!" 'Hulk' demanded.

With an annoyed sigh, Liz Wong poured her patron another Patrón shot. Why did she have to deal with such knuckleheads day after day? Why couldn't she find a respectable job, devoid of drunkards, like her friend Jenn Holtz?

Truthfully, that was kind of Liz's deal. She was a pretty typical commuter student at San Diego State, never fully immersing herself into campus life because she would take two classes in the morning and then scurry off to a job. It didn't matter that her places of employment never really matched her Business Administration major anyway, they were *jobs* and they paid the rent. She didn't really like that major anyway, but she chose it because her father had off-handedly said, "Business is a good major, and San Diego State has a good program. Why don't you study that, Elizabeth?" And she did so because she felt she owed her parents one. Tanaka and Yoshi Wong had met and married in Yokohama, Japan and immigrated to the United States. They gave their daughter, an only child, everything she could possibly ever need or want. As much as possible in their San Francisco abode, they allowed her New World experiences while still clinging to traditions from their homeland. Thus, for example, they threw her a Sweet Sixteen party and all the kids at St. Ignatius Prepatory Academy in downtown San Francisco came to celebrate their classmate. Four years later, they threw another soiree for the Japanese "Coming of Age" ceremony that Japanese families enjoy when their offspring turn 20. The Wongs attended a public ceremony for this and then feted Liz – her father always called her Elizabeth – at a lavish party in their home.

This made Liz feel slightly bad because she knew they'd want to throw *another* brilliant bash after she graduated college. Here it was 2016 and after year four of a six-year plan, she decided to take a break. Work and classes and projects and midterm exams were just too much for her. That started a string of jobs decidedly NOT related to Business Administration: being a masseuse, nanny, substitute teacher – Education was kind of a temporary backup major – and finally, bartending. These jobs were easy to get, easier to quit, and provided wonderful scheduling flexibility, if not handsome pay. Her parents hated it, hated the bouncing around from job to job (her friend Jenn always said "*jab*" in her Midwestern brogue, *jab to jab*), hated the lack of financial stability and health insurance, hated the douchebags like this one slumping at the bar.

One particularly positive development from a prior bartending job, "See the good even in negative experiences," Jenn would always say, was she met Kris. They bartended together, stayed in touch after Liz was fired for giving away too many drinks to regulars, and eventually became lovers. Theirs was a relationship that burned brightly in intensity and passion.

Arguments were fairly frequent and Liz would be the first one to tell you Kris was a more rational ying to her highly emotional yang. She knew Kris loved her and had Liz's best interests at heart. Today was a good example of that. With her shift ending, she truly wanted to spend a couple hours lounging on the beach. But a lump she had felt on her left breast changed all that.

"Don't go to the beach after you get off tomorrow!" Kris had admonished her the night before. "We live in San Diego. You can literally go to the beach all year! Go get that lump checked out!"

Those were two things Liz hated actually. Kris yelled whenever angered and literally did not know how to use the word "literally".

"Fine. Then I will literally go to the doctor," she had said in a huff. She knew, though, Kris's anger was borne out of concern, and probably fear.

Moreover, she knew it was sage advice. And though her lack of health insurance would make this an expensive, out-of-pocket visit, she walked nervously into Dr. Setoguchi's office. She liked him, he was stately with salt and pepper hair, a slender and no-nonsense Japanese man, like her father.

She earnestly didn't mind that a male would be touching her breasts because Dr. Setoguchi was all-business. A mammogram from him would include a very clinical, stern, emotionless diagnosis.

Or so she thought.

A week passed and Liz returned to the mundane. Her worry had dissolved into daily tasks like going to work, going to her second job as a dog-walker, looking for a third job, and heeding Kris's incessant requests to get her W-2's and W-9's and WD-40's or whatever, organized for filing taxes.

"We can file now, why wait?" Kris had said with agitation, remembering last year that Liz had filed for an extension and still took almost a month to file.

It was on a chilly evening, nightfall was often the only time one would feel winter in San Diego, when Liz's cell rang. It was already past five o'clock so she was surprised at the caller: Dr. Setoguchi.

"Liz, can you visit my office tomorrow?" he asked.

So she did and brought along Kris. Although Kris insisted everything would be fine, Liz figured an office visit portended bad news. If it was good news, or no news, she would have been told that over the phone. "Oh, don't be so dramatic," Kris said.

Dr. Setoguchi welcomed them into his office and threw a file folder flatly on his desk. Kris and Liz sat across from him, holding hands.

"Liz, I'm afraid the tests have returned some surprising and unfavorable results," he said, removing his glasses. "The autopsy indicates your lump is malignant."

"What does that mean?" asked Kris.

The doctor looked directly at Kris and didn't mince words: "Your girlfriend has breast cancer. I'm sorry."

Liz's eyes welled with tears.

Kris was mortified.

Opening Daze

It was a brilliant April day. A canopy of blue skies covered San Diego and the warmth of the sunshine matched the radiance of the citizenry's mood.

It was Major League Baseball's Opening Day and the place to be was beautiful Petco Park in the East Village. This was the commencing of a special season, as the Padres were set to host MLB's All-Star Game later that summer. But even without the "Midsummer Classic", and even though the home team was not projected to win very many games, the air was abuzz with excitement.

Baseball was back, and few places offered the lush green grass, shining like an emerald gem, swaying palm trees, and pristine hacienda-style towers of Petco. The ballpark had been increasingly littered with corporate signage in its 12 years, and to be sure it wasn't a cathedral of the game like Wrigley Field in Chicago; Yankee Stadium in New York; or Fenway Park in Boston. Those were historic, whereas Petco – though its name was derived from a silly-sounding but hefty corporate partnership deal – was nouveau rich. It truly was one of the most gorgeous venues in MLB – and probably all of sports.

One of its charms, as envisioned by then-owners John Moores and Larry Lucchino in the late 1990's, was its placement in the East Village meant it was surrounded by bountiful, brick-laden condominiums and offices.

This was where Fernando Guzman's law firm was located, occupying the entire third floor of a building which included an outdoor deck. This deck arched above a grassy-knolled area known as the Park at the Park. Although you couldn't see the playing field directly, the desk was incredibly *inside* the ballpark. A giant video board relayed the game action to all deck occupants.

Which is what they all were – deck occupants – on this sensational spring afternoon. Heeding Fernando's plea of "My firm is throwing a party on Opening Day and you need to come!" there they all were. Game ticket and beer in hand, looking morose but at least relaxed were jobless Teddy; husbandless Beatriz; and himself, of course, fiancée-free Freddy.

Jenn entered with Murph and introduced the group to them and two other friends, Liz and Kris. It was evident by the pink bandana atop her head, revealing some glimpses of scalp, that Liz was battling cancer.

"Guys, I know it's been a rough winter for us, but let's raise a toast to being together on Opening Day. Jenn, I'm glad you could take a day off work to join us," said Fernando as he handed out shots of Fireball.

"Uh, well, that was kinda easy," Jenn said sheepishly, "I got laid off this week. Budget cuts."

The whole group joined Jenn in looking sad.

Fernando announced, while raising his shot glass: "Dang it, I'm sorry. But that means you'll fit right in to this group. CHEERS, to Opening Day with the Wolfpack. Wolfpack hoooowl!!!"

Baseball season had begun.

Chapter 6

An All-Star Summer

Saturday evenings in San Diego belonged to the three B's: Baseball, Bub's, and Banter. The Wolfpack would convene, usually half of them for a Padres game, but ALL of them for the post-festivities at Bub's on Seventh and K Street.

They would order tots and the ones that went to the game, usually Fernando, Beatriz, and Jenn, would meet up with the ones that didn't, Teddy and Liz.

The raw emotions each one was feeling would cloak the conversation like the thick marine layer of louds hanging over the marina, Bayfront, and Petco Park. It had been only five months, after all, since the downward spiral commenced that claimed these friends' jobs, spouses, significant others, and health.

Teddy had dubbed them The Wolfpack because the original three – he, Fernando, and Beatriz – had commiserated over adversity and then eventually welcomed Jenn and Liz into the fold.

This was an interesting time of year for Action Jackson. As a football celebrity and then television sportscaster, he had attended every Major League Baseball game in a VIP or press capacity for as back as he could remember. This was the first year he was "simply a fan," a moniker he said with some resignation and regret. The regular-season games had appeal but Teddy was already thinking ahead to July. Would he be *persona non-grata* at the city's first All-Star Game since 1992?

Noticing his compadre was fairly silent during the game and now was sipping his Cognac rather slowly, Freddy inquired: "You ok, man?"

"Oh, yeah, man, I'm good," Teddy responded, waving his hand. "It's just a little hard to be at the ballpark. I used to have press credentials for the field and skybox, you know."

"My husband's firm had season tickets," Beatriz said wistfully.

"Kris and I went all the time too," chimed in Liz.

"You guys, don't make this a depressing night!" urged Jenn.

"For real," said Fernando, "y'all are the saddest bunch since The Cure."

"What?!" exclaimed Bea, "The Cure was a great band!"

"Oh they were terrible," Fernando replied, "I never understood how so many of us Hispanics liked them when there were so many other great groups around."

"Like who?" Bea asked forcefully.

"Well, what genre?" asked Teddy.

"ALL of them, any of them," was Fernando's answer.

"You know who was great?" Beatriz asked rhetorically.

All eyes were on her as she took a sip of beer, wiped away the foam, and said: "Madonna. She's better than any current female artist."

The second part of that opinion rippled through the group.

"Uh, I think Lady Gaga is better," said Liz.

"Yeah, but for sheer pipes, I'll take Christina Aguilera," submitted Jenn.

"Oh I like her," said Teddy.

"Maaaan, you only like her 'cause she's sexy," claimed Fernando.

Teddy bristled. "Well if sexiness was the main selling point, I'd have said Britney Spears."

"Which Britney, though?" inquired Liz, "teenage, pre-nervous breakdown Britney or adult, hot mama Britney?"

"That's my point," interjected Beatriz. "Madonna was the inspiration for all these chicks. Britney. Christina. Gaga."

"That don't mean she's better than them," asserted Teddy, "it just means she's older than them."

"Hey, whatever happened to Mandy Moore?" asked Fernando wistfully.

"Mandy. Moore. Wow!" Jenn replied, each word dripping with incredulousness.

"I wanna see Moore of her," cackled Teddy, reaching out for a hard dap of Fernando's knuckle.

"Oh please, she's ok," said Beatriz, rolling her eyes.

"Wait, who's Mandy Moore?" asked Liz, sheepishly.

"Uh, she was a '90s singer who was a good girl. And she could sing and act and was cute. An anti-Ke$ha," opined Teddy.

"Hey! I like Ke$ha," exclaimed Liz.

"Of course you do," said Fernando with a smirk. Actually, Fernando always smirked. This time the smirk was accompanied by a lifting of his left eyebrow.

"Why all these singers gotta be white? No love for the sistahs?" asked Teddy extending his open palm outward in feigned desperation.

"Like.....Beyonce?" offered Liz.

"Yeah, that's one," asserted Teddy.

"Well I love Janet Jackson," said Fernando.

"And if we're talkin' pipes, who had a better voice than Whitney Houston?" mused Beatriz.

"Actually, Beyonce's younger sister Solange has a great voice too," said Jenn, "she's just not as well known."

"Could be worse," cracked Fernando, "she could be the LaToya of that family."

Said Teddy: "Or worse. At least we know who LaToya Jackson is. But no one remembers Reby."

At this the entire group burst out laughing. Fernando loved this. His Wolfpack had somehow developed a custom where togetherness bred sadness; followed by whimsical yet impassioned debates; ultimately ending up in laughter.

The Stars Come Out

Summertime reached its midpoint. July in San Diego creeps up on you because, unlike a Chicago or New York, the spring seldom includes freezing temperatures or deluges of rain and thunder. May is mostly mild and June conspicuously arrives with thick marine layer dubbed as "June Gloom" by locals. July, really, isn't noticed until there are a plethora of Independence Day fireworks and barbeques.

A different type of gloom, however, had settled in among the pack.

San Diego, though the weather is pleasant year-round, is a summer town. There are annual events that only occur in the summer and they become a part of people's lives. A rite of passage, traditions either handed down or enjoyed individually with your social group.

Some are fairly banal, like afternoons broiling at the beach or bronzing in backyard swimming pools. Other traditions are more specific, like the County Fair; with its location of seaside resort town Del Mar, historically it was called the Del Mar Fair until the last decade or so when the powers-that-be officially changed the name to "San Diego County Fair." San Diegans, though mostly comprised of transplants, had a thing about tradition. Jack Murphy Stadium, though its name changed in 1997, was still regarded as The Murph. (Jenn's boyfriend loved that and claimed it was named after him.) The County Fair, ergo, was still the Del Mar Fair to most.

In that same city were horse races, held after the Fair shut down for the year on the Fourth of July, and extending into September, when students scurry back to school and the beaches and zoo and parks are far more desolate.

Part of the charm of these traditions – playing hooky and guzzling beer at the races or enjoying a sunlit afternoon at the Fair or Padres game – is that couples can enjoy them. And for those in the Wolfpack that were no longer a part of a couple, wistfulness abounded.

Beatriz mournfully recounted how she and her ex would spend Sunday summer nights down in the adjoining community of Coronado – which was actually an island – listening to live classical music and strolling through the mostly retiree-populated streets, one hand holding an ice cream cone and the other interlocking fingers with her man.

Fernando would come home from work and suddenly realize he had a whole lot of daylight left and no one to share it with. It was the summer sunsets he and Katie would enjoy most, sometimes sipping wine from his balcony and other times walking around the Gaslamp Quarter and enjoying the collection of lights, exuberant voices, and neon-colored clothing, all surrounded by balmy air.

Liz, as the summer of 2016, arrived had sadness too. She missed Kris fiercely, that relationship having soured amid the worry and mounting medical bills with her illness. This was Kris's birthday month too, a milestone they annually celebrated with impromptu drives up Highway One to San Francisco or hopping a flight to Vegas for the weekend.

Jenn was feeling sadness *and* worry. She had been laid off from her job and subsequently fell into a funk. Murph didn't quite know what to say or how to pull her out of it, which led to increased mutual resentment and bickering. They weren't quite broken up but they were growing more and more distant. Her mother was also not doing well, her Multiple Sclerosis rendering her quite feeble, slow afoot, with dimming vision. It was hard to remain cheerful and optimistic.

Knowing all of these emotions existed, including his own, and that his sometime-buddy and sometime-competitor, especially for women, Teddy was blue about not having press credentials to the Major League Baseball All-Star Game at Petco Park, Fernando had an idea.

He gathered the crew one Friday night at Basic Pizza and declared: "Guys, the All-Star Game is coming to town. And whether you have a significant other or not, or a press pass or not, dang it, I'm gonna make sure we all enjoy it! You know what I'm gonna do?"

"Sneak us in?" asked Liz.

"No." Fernando stated.

"Jump on the field and go streaking?" Jenn asked, sounding eerily hopeful.

"What? No!"

"Get hammered?" asked Teddy.

"No!" Fernando responded. "Well, maybe."

"Guys, my office overlooks the outfield at Petco Park," Fernando explained, gesticulating like he was trying to convince a jury. "I'm gonna make sure all of you experiences the All-Star Game, if even from slightly afar. I'm throwing a party!"

The mid-July air was warm but not suffocating. J Street in the East Village was crammed with baseball fans from San Diego to Saratoga, from California to Connecticut, from the Pacific to the projects back East. It was a congress of fanatics, all there to celebrate the players chosen for the All-Star Game but ostensibly to support the sport itself. The beauty of baseball is that, although it's the American pastime, it is now a truly international sport, with players hailing from Japan, Puerto Rico, the Dominican Republic, Mexico, Canada, Korea, Venezuela, and of course, the good ol' United States.

In his office loft outside the Petco Park outfield, Fernando's guests, clients and friends alike, weren't as keenly interested in the players' backgrounds as they were in making sure they had tickets and enough beer.

"I can't believe I'm this close to the beauty that is Buster Posey," gushed the Bay Area native Liz.

"Come on, he's not even the best player here," chided Teddy.

"Who is?" Liz asked, knowing she was girding for a fight.

"Mike Trout," Teddy affirmed with confidence.

"Well neither one of those guys holds a candle to my all-time favorite, Fernando Valenzuela," said Freddy, invoking his namesake.

"Come on, man," Teddy said, rolling his eyes, "1981 called and they want their All-Star back."

Across the room, Beatriz was chatting with a handsome young work associate of Fernando's. Both Fernando and Teddy pretended to not notice, but they noticed.

So did Liz and Jenn when Bea sauntered back to the group.

"Who was THAT?" they asked in unison.

Teddy, leaning against a wall nearby, rolled his eyes again. "Oh geez, what a bunch of schoolgirls," he said.

Fernando sipped his red solo cup and inwardly agreed with Action Jackson, but knew that his buddy was more agitated than usual. He surmised it was because Teddy was not on the field, hob-knobbing with David Ortiz and Clayton Kershaw and Kris Bryant and other baseball luminaries. He was right. Simply being a fan was not easy for Teddy. It wasn't so much not cavorting with pro athletes, it was that *his* colleagues were on the field, building memories they could post immediately on social media and re-live forever in future happy hours.

"Oh, just a friend," answered Beatriz lightly.

"Well did he ask you out?" inquired Liz.

"Actually," replied Bea with a faint smile, "we've gone out. A couple times."

"What? When were you gonna say something? I've been texting you now for months," said Teddy, in a rather impatient tone.

"And I've taken you to dinner and coffee and stuff," said Fernando.

"You have??" asked Liz and Jenn in unison.

Beatriz did not like the sudden cross-examination. "Uh, yes, and since when do I have to report to you guys every time I go out with a guy?"

"So there's been other times?" Fernando persisted, with his eyebrows raised and mouth ajar.

"Shut up you guys, I have to take this," Jenn said suddenly, grabbing her cell phone.

She retreated to a nearby, quieter corner. The group didn't pay her any mind until they heard these words come from her mouth:

"What? No! Noooooooooo! I'll....I'll....oh my gash......I'll be right there."

She hung her phone up and burst into tears.

Chapter 7

Vegas, Baby

The funeral for Jenn's mother was on a sunlit Friday morning. There were no marine-layer clouds that late July day but an air of heaviness hung over the outdoor services.

With Southern California largely being devoid of humidity, it was not too uncomfortable wearing black clothes. Not that anyone in the Wolfpack minded anyway, their affection for Jenn was such that they all wanted to be there for her, even if the day had included searing heat, stifling air, and oppressive humidity. But it did not, which was one bright in an otherwise somber day.

The men wore black suits and the ladies donned black dresses. Some wore large-brimmed hats or fedoras. Everyone wore sunglasses. But even the darkest pair of shades could not mask Jenn's puffy eyes or tears streaming down her freckled cheeks.

Her mother was more than just her creator of life. She was her confidante, encourager, and constant reminder that everything was going to be fine. Keep doing good in this world, she'd tell her daughter, the world won't appreciate it but do good anyway. You are a difference maker.

How could this happen? How could life be so cruel? There are so many bad, ill-intentioned people in the world and one that gets taken is a truly good, kind-hearted one?

In one respect, Jenn was glad her mother was finally free of the pain and struggle her Multiple Sclerosis had thrust upon her. It had been a long time since she could see clearly or walk with ease. It just wasn't fair. But now she could join Papa in heaven, who had passed from cancer when Jenn was barely a wide-eyed ten-year old. Plus she'd join Nana and Paw-Paw, each of whom went to be with the Lord when she was in high school and college, respectively. She started to feel like life was playing the ultimate diabolical joke on her, slowly taking anyone that mattered to her. "Don't feel that way, sweetie," her mother had said, "life IS unfair. But don't ask *WHY ME? ASK WHY NOT ME?* The Lord never gives us more than we can handle."

Sage advice. But now the purveyor of those words was gone too.

At the reception at the house her mother had lived in, Jenn summoned the strength to be a gracious host. She pleasantly thanked guests for coming and smiled as bravely as possible. The Wolfpack chipped in too, according to their talents and personalities. Fernando helped greet people, not because he had any official connection to the family, but because his persona was to welcome folks, ask where they were from, and listen patiently to their stories. Liz and Beatriz served crackers, diced fruit, and established a tandem of bringing one tray into the living room and marching another one out. Jenn's family had a wet-bar on the back patio and Murph served as bartender. He didn't really deal well with sad moments – what do you say to people to console their grief? – so he tried to keep the mood light without being seemingly inappropriate. Speaking of being inappropriate, whoever was in a short black skirt warranted Teddy's attention. Until Jenn leaned over while he was on the couch, chatting with a 21-year old cousin of hers from Santa Barbara, and whispered in a sharp tone: "STOP hitting on my cousins – or any women in here! Or I will kick you in the balls!"

Teddy nearly spit out his bourbon upon hearing that last part, but he knew not to challenge Jenn. He edged away from the couch.

Whether gatherings are happy or mournful, they eventually end. This one did too and with it ended Jenn's need to be preoccupied with being a good host. Reality set in with the oncoming days and with it came a moroseness for the crestfallen daughter.

Her mother was gone. Her job was gone. Her motivation was gone.

She barely slept at night, leading to drowsy afternoons. Her appetite was non-existent. All of the causes and busyness that she would update her mother on, and in turn get updates from her mom on *her* passion projects, didn't seem important anymore.

Murph didn't know how to deal with this depression. Should he offer encouraging words and risk getting snapped at? Should he offer consoling words and tenderness, and if so, would she believe this departure from his generally brusque demeanor? What should he do?

This period of mourning impacted the group too in that they unofficially took a break from hanging out. A sadness had pervaded them and it just didn't seem right that they get together while Jenn was deeply depressed.

As August loomed, Murph tried to shake his girlfriend out of her doldrums. "Babe, I know you're hurting, but you have to move on," he implored. "Life goes on and you have to move forward. Your mother would want that!"

Jenn simply sat on her couch, draped in a pink bathrobe and ensconced in sadness.

Rolling the Dice

It was a balmy Wednesday night and August had just begun. Like someone lighting a fuse, Fernando sent a mass text-message to Jenn, Liz, Bea, Teddy, and Murph: *We need to get away. Vegas. This wknd. I'll drive.*

The responses ranged from LOL to OMG to Jenn's simple but heartfelt *Sorry, just not ready.*

To which Fernando responded: *Jenn with two n's, we luv u. You need this. WE need this. Wolfpack hoooowl!!!*

This made Jenn chuckle privately and the rest of the crew exclaim via text: *YES! Let's do it! I'm in!*

Fernando went on to explain he had some unused points at Mandalay Bay in Las Vegas, and could cash them in for a suite for two nights. If he drove – a suburban truck that could fit everyone - all people had to do was chip in for gas. This was a no-brainer, easily the cheapest getaway offer they'd ever receive. The Saharan dessert temps of late summer were less than desirous, but…Fernando was right. The Wolfpack needed a road trip to get away from the rigors of life.

Jenn's thumbs lit the fuse further: *Vegas, baby. Let's roll.*

A stream of responses flurried:

Alright!
Boom!
Holla!
Dope!
Shotgun!
Vegas, baby.

The fighting began somewhere between Barstow and Zzyzx – a true name for an unincorporated area formerly known as Camp Soda. Somewhere along the way it was re-named Zzyx, which was not only quirky but generally brought joy because seeing the Zzyzx sign indicates Las Vegas is not too far away.

Joy was something Fernando hoped would come quick. His friends were bickering like schoolkids or spoiled teenagers. He and Jenn took on an almost parental role because she volunteered to ride shotgun and be a co-navigator. Murph was fine with that because he could ride in the far back, recline, and steadfastly nap. In the middle aisle were the three kids, er, passengers – Teddy, Liz, and Beatriz – who didn't take long to torment Fernando and Jenn.

They had left San Diego in the late morning, excited and brimming with anticipation, and drove about two hours. Although Jenn had plied the group with road trip snacks – beef jerky, cashews, Gatorade, Sour Strings, crackers, waters, granola bars – they didn't eat too much, partially because Fernando had said, "If I see crumbs on my leather upholstery, I will fight you."

Eventually Jenn's urging of, "Freddy, let's at least go to a drive-through for lunch" resonated with Fernando's hunger pangs, counteracting his need to drive fast, steady, and efficient. He had promised to get the group to Nevada in under five hours, to which Teddy replied, "Bruh, what's the rush? Everything in Vegas is open 24/7 – including the ladies."

That elicited a hard punch to his left shoulder from Liz Wong.

As lunchtime neared, Fernando called out, "What are we having that's tasty and won't mess up my car?"

The suggestions came like Fernando's favorite movie and driving style: *Fast and Furious.*

Teddy: Mickey D.'s!

Liz: Burger King!

Jenn: Somewhere organic. Oh! Let's find a Whole Foods!

Beatriz: Chic Fil-A!

Murph: KFC!

Fernando rolled his eyes and said, "Then it's settled. I'm stopping at the next Taco Bell I see. Cheap and easy – like Teddy on a Saturday night."

The pack howled with laughter. Teddy grimaced.

After lunch, another important decision needed to be finalized. Fernando called out, "Jenn is in charge of the Pandora. What music station should she choose?"

And in the words of Tears for Fears, *Everybody Wants to Rule the World.*

Murph: House of Pain!

Beatriz: Selena!

Liz: Dixie Chicks!

Teddy: New Edition!

Jenn: Taylor Swift!

"Then that settles it," declared Fernando, "for the next four hours we're listening to Jay-Z!"

The group groaned. Fernando, being the master litigator and negotiator turned to Jenn and said, "Just put it on shuffle. If a song is slow, just skip to the next one, no matter the genre."

Jenn responded with a thumbs-up salute. When she initially met Fernando, she thought him to be a bit arrogant, but lately she was starting to admire his ability to think on his feet and have the entire group's happiness in mind when making a decision or even a suggestion. She wished she could be more forthright like that.

On the horizon, there it lay, like a shimmering jewel. The Las Vegas skyline beckoned in the sweltering late afternoon sun. The casinos, towering restaurants, and luxury hotels all stood in welcoming fashion. The Mirage was a mirage.

Liz was as excited as a kid entering Disneyland: "I've never been here as an adult! Let's go to the Palms! Oooh and Ghost Bar! Ooh and the Playboy Club!"

"*Tranquilo, tranquilo,*" Fernando said to calm Liz's giddiness. "Let's check in to Mandalay Bay first and then follow the plan."

"Which is?" Jenn asked, as they parked.

"To have no plan. That's Vegas, baby," Fernando said grinning.

With the Wolfpack, everyone had individual needs and preferences. In a fatherly yet not overbearing way, Fernando told everyone they were certainly welcome to do as they pleased, but the objective here was to do fun group activities. Therefore everyone's situation would be considered.

Liz Wong was in the early stages of radiation, so sun exposure was not good, plus she tired easier and earlier than the others. Teddy "Action" Jackson didn't need, but did love, the chance to do some sports betting – heck, he wasn't a sportscaster anymore so there was no conflict of interest or fear of reprisal. Beatriz requested activities that didn't remind her of her estranged husband so no restaurants with romantic views or nightclubs where people coupled up. Murph was perfectly happy at the craps tables and said, "I don't need to see no weak Blue Man's Group or fruity Chippendales."

This annoyed Jenn but Freddy said, "Just roll with it. What matters is we're all together by the end of the night."

Atop the Palms was the world-famous Ghost Bar. The glass flooring allowed club revelers to look down the 55 floors onto the Vegas ground level. This was part of the outdoor patio and not for the faint of heart or anyone with a fear of heights.

Across the walkway, past the bartender and DJ booth teeming with song requestors and disc jockey groupies, was the inside part of the club.

A commotion caught Fernando's eye. He tapped Teddy on the shoulder and pointed toward one of the VIP booths. "Yo, man," said Fernando, "I know I'm pretty faded right now, but isn't that Jay Cutler walking in?"

Teddy replied, "Jay Cutler, the Chicago Bears quarterback?"

"No, knucklehead, Jay Cutler the opera singer. Of course Jay Cutler, the Bears quarterback, foo'!" Fernando chided.

Teddy squinted and said, "Freddy, my man, you're right. That's Jay Cutler – wow. I've interviewed him before, he'll recognize me. Let's go say hi."

"Oooh, I wanna come! I hate the Bears but that's ok," piped in the Packer-loving Jenn. She grabbed Murph's arm. He was ambivalent about seeing Cutler but was always intrigued whenever he saw a professional athlete in person.

Liz and Bea stayed on the dance floor. The music called for some serious booty-shaking. Beatriz was reserved – her parents always derided scantily-clad women on TV if they danced too sensually – but then Liz handed her a shot of Fireball. It went down hot and cinnamon-y and immediately Bea felt her hips loosen and an involuntary smile crossed her face. The duo danced while many male onlookers peered at them.

Cutler entered the VIP area slowly. It was obvious he and a buddy – every celebrity has a manager or assistant who joins him for nights out – were waiting for the club security to lead the way.

"That's his Turtle," observed Teddy.

"His what?" asked Fernando, while Jenn and Murph looked at him in equal confusion.

"His Turtle," Teddy explained, "like the character 'Turtle' from the TV show *Entourage*. Every celebrity, especially athletes, has a friend he pays to be his assistant. They go everywhere with these guys. See? His Turtle just pointed out which VIP booth they want."

The burly bouncers led the duo to a private booth and then roped it off as a gaggle of short-skirted female employees covered the table with a bucket of ice, a tray of Grey Goose vodka bottles, and multiple glasses – presumably if Cutler invited guests into the booth.

Teddy brought the crew close enough to where Cutler could see them. He then shouted out, "Hey Jay! Jay! It's me, Action Jack---!"

Suddenly he felt a hand placed across his chest, like a big paw. It was one of the security guards, who said, "Mr. Cutler doesn't want any autograph seekers."

Chuckling, Teddy replied, "Oh I don't want an autograph. I was a journalist. I just want to say hel--..."

The bouncer, wearing an earpiece device, was firmer in his follow-up: "Mr. Cutler doesn't want any guests. I don't care who you are, brotha."

"Oh, so now we're brothers?" asked Teddy, indignantly, of his fellow African-American counterpart.

"Teddy," Fernando interjected, "it's cool, man, don't waste your time on a mediocre quarterback and his lackeys."

Another bouncer stepped in. "Who you calling a lackey, son?"

Realizing the situation could quickly escalate, Murph started gently pushing his friends away, to get them all moving away from the booth area. Then he heard a cantankerous shriek. It was his girlfriend, Jenn, who shouted: "Screw you, Jay Cutler! Packers rule, Bears drool! And you, you... you throw like a GIRL!"

Cutler glanced over and smirked, which was always part of his smarmy persona, an ever-present smirk.

The foursome edged away and Murph knew Jenn was half-inebriated, half fired up, as she kept yelling: "Screw you, Cutler! Screw you!"

They scooped Liz and Bea from the dance floor. Security asked them to leave.

"Easy, girl," Fernando said to Jenn with a smile, "it's nearly sunrise. Let's all go eat."

Murph was embarrassed and livid at his normally sweet Jenn. The rest of the Wolfpack laughed as they stumbled out of the casino lobby.

They walked down the Strip, past the towering fountains of the Bellagio, past the abundance of call girls winking at Teddy and Freddy, past the soaring roller coaster of New York New York, and past the clanging of coin machines everywhere they went. Even at dawn, with the sun barely peering above the desert skyline, it was an oppressive heat.

They stumbled into the MGM Grand, where a breakfast buffet was being served. Though normally vociferous, the group was now quiet, an amalgam of drowsiness, voracious hunger, and individual pensiveness.

Murph was thinking about the volatility of Jenn's behavior lately. She was mourning the loss of her mother and still depressed about being laid off. On a good day she'd rebound with maximum optimism but then sadness would pervade her again. Was this relationship worth the yo-yo of emotions?

Jenn was sensing she needed to change *something* about her life. Perhaps a change of scenery or direction. She was tired of being tired. She knew she was a big challenge to Murph these days. Something had to give.

Fernando glanced at Jenn as he cut into his steak and eggs. Man, she looked smokin' tonight (this morning?) or was that the Red Bulls and vodka talking? The good thing was this was the first female, aside from a brief flirtation with Beatriz, to give him feelings since Katie.

Liz really missed Kris. Undergoing radiation treatments alone was not easy. Some people, though, just can't handle the uncertainty and downright fear of potentially losing a loved one. That fear turns into detachment. Liz was crushed.

The only one that really was going through a positive, yet still gradual, metamorphosis was Teddy. The All-Star Game came and went and he was ok. He was realizing sports, whether it was him as an athlete or broadcaster, didn't define him. It was a page that could be turned and he could still be a fan. He was even hitting on fewer younger women.

Teddy raised his glass suddenly. Though his voice was hoarse from shouting in the club, he meagerly managed a toast: "To the Wolfpack. I love you guys."

Chapter 8

The Fall

The Sunday sunshine shone bright as ever. But there was a tinge of crispness in the air. And with it, some sadness too. As much as they had bonded over the past ten months, individually there were still problems and pain in their lives.

All of those were pushed aside, however, for at least three hours each Sunday. To everyone's surprise, Beatriz revealed an unknown passion of hers: Dallas Cowboys football.

This was unleashed on the drive home from Vegas, turning an otherwise groggy, low-energy, hangover-infused car ride into – what else? – a lively debate. The Wolfpack had started talking about upcoming fall activities and Teddy immediately noted football season was coming up. His teams were basically whoever he had played for, including the Chargers.

"Maaaan, forget the Chargers," Fernando chided him, "they're bad and don't even wanna be here. You know they're leaving San Diego after the season, right?"

"Man, don't say that, there's still time to work out a stadium deal," Teddy insisted, glancing over at Fernando in the driver's seat.

Everyone then chimed in with who was their team, and it was mostly a repeat of old declarations. Murph also loved the Chargers; Jenn was a Packers fan; and Liz supported the 49ers. Then a tiny voice emerged.

"Please. It's all about the Cowboys," Beatriz said proudly.

Everyone silenced and turned their heads to her. They had never heard her mention sports, save for the occasional Padres game for social reasons, let alone claim allegiance to a specific team. What was even odder was this was not a local team like the Bolts or Pads, or even a regional one, like the Lakers or Kings or Dodgers or Angels.

How 'bout them Cowboys?

Bea could see the confusion on the crew's faces so she explained, "My grandfather was from Texas, so he watched their games growing up. And even out here – well, California – my daddy watched Cowboys games with me. It was how we bonded."

Fernando could certainly understand THAT.

Beatriz added, smiling and hunching her shoulders together: "I had a crush on Troy Aikman."

Fernando could NOT relate to THAT.

So there they were on the first weekend of September, in a corner booth at Bub's, which by now may as well have been dubbed "The Wolfpack Booth". The entire bar was primarily fixated on two teams – the Chargers, the local outfit, and the Cowboys, the polarizing love-'em-or-hate-'em iconic national team. Even the Wolfpackers rooting for the Chargers would pay attention to how the 'Boys were doing, to either support or chastise their beloved Beatriz.

"TJ, why you so quiet today, man?" Fernando asked in his backwards baseball cap and Sunday scruff.

Teddy was also casual, which for him meant a Tommy Bahama button-down shirt, pressed khaki shorts, and matching brown sandals. He replied, "Oh, I just miss the game, man. It's hard enough not playing but to not be covering any of it either....man, they really screwed me."

"Who screwed you?" Fernando asked, before sipping his Budweiser.

"The TV station, bro," Teddy replied, rather incredulously.

Everyone at the booth grew silent but Fernando didn't hold back. "Teddy, you were busted for drunk driving, man, that was a decision made by YOU."

Teddy was clearly agitated. He replied, "Don't you think I know that, man? But it was my first mistake. Couldn't I get a warning or something?"

Fernando leaned in now, also annoyed. "Teddy, they warned you about hitting on younger women. They warned you about making political statements on the air. You drove drunk and could have killed someone else or yourself!"

Jenn grabbed Fernando's arm. He knew she was trying to calm him down and testily said, "No, I'm tired of it, you guys. We get together to have a good time, not just here, but Mardi Gras, St. Patty's Day, the All-Star Game, Vegas, whatever. And this guy mopes! Now, I know what it's like to have loss, but this guy blames everyone but himself!"

"Oh, wow, ok, I see how it is, Mr. Perfect," said Teddy, pushing aside his Jack and Coke. "What about you, huh? You don't think you're at fault either? I've heard you talking about Katie leaving you and you know what stands out to me, man? You never listened to her. You did what YOU thought was right for the relationship. You never asked her. And she left you 'cause of it."

Fernando stood up and assumed a physically intimidating, ready-to-fight position. Teddy readied to reciprocate.

"You guys, stop it!" Liz shouted.

The entire bar, including the bouncers, were watching now. Fernando just shook his head, threw a 20-dollar bill on the table to cover his tab, and angrily stormed off. Teddy quietly laughed, though he felt a mixture of regret and hurt. Jenn slid out from the booth, dodged some bystanders who were staring at her foam cheesehead, and chased after Fernando.

Murph called out, "Jenn, what are you doing? Where you goin'?"

Teddy said, "Forget those two. Forget that guy."

WHOOOOO-HOOOOOO! A shout pierced the air. It was Beatriz. Rookie Ezekiel Elliott had just scored a touchdown for Dallas. How 'bout them Cowboys?

The spat between Freddy and Teddy had some unintended consequences. For one, it mutually opened up wounds that had not quite closed yet. Also, because these two – plus the outspoken Liz – were really the "leaders of the pack" there was a ripple effect. Text threads about the latest controversial statement by Trump or who would eventually go to the Super Bowl or who the coolest character was in *Saved by the Bell* – Fernando and Jenn led the Team Zach contingent, while Bea advocated for Team Screetch – were non-existent. Because two members were not talking, the entire Wolfpack was not talking.

One week led to two weeks. Two weeks led to three. Beatriz watched the Cowboys games at Bub's with maybe a Jenn here or a Liz there.

Finally Liz had had enough. When two adults aren't mature enough to engage in conversation, she knew she still had technology on her side. She grabbed her phone one gray, early October day and wrote a mass-text to everyone in the Wolfpack.

It read:

TO: FREDDY, TEDDY, BEA, JENN, MURPH

Alright, kids, I know Fernando & Teddy r still being hurt little snowflakes, but I feel I must remind you of something. One thing this Wolfpack always does is celebrate birthdays. Well, my bday is coming up & it's my 1st without Kris in a long time. If u can afford it, I wanna do a trip to Chicago and if the Cubs r still in the playoffs, I want 2 go to a game!"

"Dang it," said Teddy, upon reading the text.

"Awwww," said Beatriz, who responded with a thumbs up and a flurry of hearts.

"Ay, caramba," said Fernando.

"Wish I could, kid," Murph wrote back, "work has got me by the balls but we'll celebrate when u get back."

Jenn, however, dissented from her boyfriend, responding: "YAAAAASSS! I need this and you boyz def need this. Let's book our flights & hotels 2DAY."

So in late October, the Wolfpack headed to one of the greatest cities in the world, Chicago.

Chicago in the fall is not just a delight, it is a magnificent experience. The golden embers of sunshine matching the brown and gold leaves; the abundance of boots and jackets and scarves being worn on Michigan Avenue; the smell of hot dogs wafting through the Second City air. Unfortunately, tensions between Fernando and Teddy made things as icy as the biting wind swirling throughout downtown. This was Liz's birthday and she was NOT having that.

Her actual birthday fell on their first full day in town, so Liz made a request: let's make sure we're out at midnight so we can raise a beer toast at the stroke of twelve. The group agreed and also consented to her venue of choice: the Cubbie Hole in Wrigleyville. The Wolfpack wanted to scout the area out before buying playoff tickets on StubHub two days later, and whereas that day they'd be INSIDE Wrigley Field, this was their chance to enjoy the surroundings OUTSIDE "The Friendly Confines". They took group photos and selfies outside the home plate marquee and bought t-shirts from a street vendor who lamented, "Oh my gash, I can't believe you's guys are from San Diego. That ball rolling through Leon Durham's legs broke my heart. That was Ack-tober 1984 and it's da' worse memory I gat."

Liz also had ulterior motives. She knew a night of refreshments and Chicago dogs – no ketchup allowed, Teddy recalled from his upbringing in nearby South Bend – would make it hard for the two squabbling sirs to stay upset. Let's get this kissing and making up out of the way early, she thought.

Kissing was also on the mind of Jenn. What was WRONG with her? Sure, her and Murph were really struggling with their relationship since she was laid off and her mom went to be with the Lord. But her depression, thanks to some good prescription drugs and therapy, had lessened. So why was she noticing how utterly good Fernando looked in his black jacket and matching beanie? He resembled a young Enrique Iglesias. Jenn shook her head forcefully and pushed away her tall-boy can of Natural Light.

"Hi, guys, I'm your new server now, you wanna another Natty Light?" asked a young, perky, auburn-haired, freckled-faced server.

"And what's YOUR name?" Teddy asked in his customary, suave tone.

"Ugh," Freddy murmured under his breath.

The server extended her right arm for a handshake. "Everyone here calls me Sully, or you can call me by my first name – Katie."

"Ugh!" said Fernando even louder. Hearing the same name as his ex-fiancee was as distasteful as the onions on a Chicago dog. Jenn immediately sensed this and ordered a round of shots for the table.

Katie – or 'Sully' – laughed and said, "Gat it. Round of shats. I'll add it yer ta-ab."

The Wolfpack drank and played pool and shuffleboard and sang aloud to tunes like *Wonder Wall* and *Runaround*, until *Closing Time* by '90's one-hit wonder Semisonic provided a perfect karaoke-like conclusion. They toasted Liz at midnight and WERE toasted by 12:02.

Teddy then felt a tinge of remorse and put his arm around the nape of Fernando's neck. "Freddy, I'm sorry, man, I shouldn't have come atchu like that, man. That's my bad and you're right, bro, I need to own up to my mistakes too," he said.

Fernando winced and replied, "No, no, I was too harsh, man. And you're right, I need to accept that Katie left me because I was too pushy. I need to just back off ALL women from now on."

Teddy laughed and said, "Appreciated, man, but don't be hasty. There's ONE woman that obviously likes you."

Fernando was perplexed. Teddy smiled and nodded toward a young woman throwing darts affixed to a picture of Donald Trump. She was giggling, high-fiving her female friends, and then glanced directly at Fernando.

It was Jenn. With two n's and one gleam in her eye.

The next two days were spent enjoying the aptly-named Magnificent Mile, Sears Tower, and Michael Jordan Steakhouse. The group made silly poses at the Bean and bought copious amounts of sneakers at Nike Town. Teddy broke away for lunch with some cousins in the South Side and then reconvened with the Pack back on Waveland Avenue at dusk.

There they enjoyed being part of a hopeful masse of people, cheering lustily for the Cubs to reach their first World Series since 1945. If they advanced that far, the Cubbies had an opportunity for their first world championship since 1908. It was a streak of futility unparalleled in sports. It was even immortalized at another pub they'd visited that day in downtown, the Billy Goat Tavern – so named because legend had it the owner tried to take a billy goat into that '45 World Series and was rebuffed. The ensuing anger over the rejection led to a stated hex on the North Side nine that forever cemented them as Lovable Losers. The tavern had newspaper accounts about The Curse plastered all over its walls, along with a sign that read CHEEZEBOIGER, CHEEZEBOIGER, CHEEZEBOIGER. It was a homage to their Greek-immigrant owner whose insistence in the 1970's on stubbornly *telling* people what to eat (and drink) belied the toughness of Chicago. John Belushi then recreated that on Saturday Night Live.

Chicago was a city of broad shoulders, bifurcated between the North and South Side, and intensely segregated, not just by race, but by groups of various ethnicities and countries. It had overcome Mrs. O'Leary's cow tipping over a lantern that started a massive fire, riots in the 1968

Democratic National Convention, the cheating of the Black Sox scandal, obscene political corruption, and of course, the Cubs' hapless existence.

On this night they won and were marching toward the World Series. Liz was ecstatic to celebrate her birthday in this fashion and compared Chi-town's resilience to that of her beloved Wolfpack's strength. She was perplexed though, why the Major League Baseball schedule-makers had the Fall Classic, heretofore entrenched in October, concluding in November.

"It may snow during the World Series!" Liz lamented in an ultra-surprised tone.

"Well," said Fernando, gazing at Jenn, who was staring right back at him, "anything is possible."

Howl-a-ween

The chilly air was enshrouded by a nighttime mist. It was Halloween in the East Village and as Ghetto Boys once said in a 1990's rap song: "This year / Halloween fell on a weekend / Me and Ghetto Boys / went trick-or-treatin'". The Wolfpack didn't go to trick or treat, but they did have candy in mind – eye candy. And the East Village provided plenty of that.

They met up at Quartyard, an outdoor bar on the epicenter street of Market Street and Tenth Avenue. It was located in an old parking lot, which was converted into a watering hole by installing tables, benches, food trucks, and of course, a large bar.

They each showed up in their costumes. Fernando was a fireman; Teddy embraced his retired sportsman's motif by dressing as newly retired pro quarterback Peyton Manning; Jenn and Murph were a cowboy and cowgirl. Beatriz was a naughty angel – an outfit she felt impeccably guilty about wearing, but for years she avoided donning the sexy costumes many women wear at Halloween. This was her time to take a risk and wear such flirty attire.

Liz, however, opted for a more political statement. Republican presidential candidate Donald Trump had caused a social firestorm by being overheard on a discarded 2005 B-roll of an interview bragging about how he enjoyed "grabbing women by the pussy." So she wore an all-black ensemble of leggings and a t-shirt, attached a headband with cat ears atop it, and tucked into the back of her pants a long striped, orange and black cat tail. Kris would've probably asked, "How the heck are you going to sit on that thing?" But, alas, Kris was gone, having left their relationship amid emotions of fear over Liz's radiation treatments.

That weighed heavily on Liz, who always went big on Halloween costumes but was clearly unhappy to be there tonight. She missed Kris.

The group, though, quickly pounced on the opportunity to make a twisted joke. "Hey, Liz," Freddy called out while grabbing a mug of his favorite pale ale, "bring your cat paws over here. Let's take a picture for Snap-Chat. Just you, me, and Teddy. We are the MEN O' PAWS. Get it, like menopause?"

"Ewwwwww," said Beatriz.

"That's gross, man," noted Murph.

"It is gross. But I like it," said Liz, handing Jenn her Samsung phone – she refused to get an iPhone like everyone else – to take a picture.

As the photo clicked, Teddy borrowed from his reborn pal Fernando and shouted, "Wolfpack hooooowl! Men 'o' puse power, baby!"

Nearby strangers were puzzled and disgusted by that. The Wolfpack didn't care.

The night was a gradual procession of geography and drinks. They bar-hopped and enjoyed the streams of people walking about in their costumes. Slutty and sexy nurses; macabre men with meat cleavers attached to their (fake) bloodied t-shirts; more politically-oriented costumes like a Trump lookalike arresting a Hillary Clinton clone – both with blonde wigs – with handcuffs, as he promised to do on the campaign trail. Murph loved that one, Teddy did not.

The Wolfpack enjoyed a window seat at the Knotty Barrel, which afforded them a stoop similar to an East Coast apartment patio. They took shots of Fireball and tequila at The Blind Burro. And, of course, they wound up at Bub's.

This was earnestly the first night Jenn and Murph were not bickering in a while. Fernando was happy that Jenn was happy, but couldn't honestly say that made him *happy*. Really this was the best night – outside of Chicago – the group had in a while.

Except, quite evidently, for Beatriz. "Bea, what's wrong?" Fernando asked, upon noticing her dejected expression in their Bub's booth.

"Oh, I just don't like Halloween," she explained, "I mean, I *like* it, and I'm glad I'm finally free to wear a costume like this that my parents definitely would hate. But my ex has the kids this weekend. I just wish I was trick-or-treating with them."

"I feel you, sister," said a drunk and downcast Liz, "Kris and I did matching outfits every year. We usually threw a party too."

"Well, my situation's a little tougher," Beatriz noted. She paused and sighed.

The group all had their eyes on her.

"He's asked to have full custody of the kids."

The sentiments of disgust were in unison: *What?! No way! Fight him all the way!*

Bea replied, "Thanks, you guys. Losing him to another woman was hard. But what if I lose my *kids*?"

Tears were streaming down Beatriz's eyes.

Chapter 9

Crisis

November 9 dawned like so many other San Diego days. A sunrise encircled in pink hues, emblazoned with dark gray clouds on the perimeter and a canopy of baby blue skies surrounding it. If you were at one of the cities many beaches – such as Mission, Ocean, La Jolla, or Coronado Beach – such a beautiful sight intermingled with the intoxicating smell of the salt water and the screetches of sea gulls could be heavenly.

But Teddy Jackson was not at the beach. He was in his overpriced condominium in downtown San Diego and he was depressed. He was stoic. He was stunned. Needing somewhere to go, he threw on a pair of dingy gray sweat pants and a gray t-shirt, with NOTRE DAME FOOTBALL emblazoned across the chest and headed outside. He walked toward the nearest East Village coffee shop, forcefully yet aimlessly.

It was so quiet it was deafening.

The previous day was Election Day in America.

And America, as Teddy feared she would do, yet truly didn't think was a viable possibility, elected Donald J. Trump as President of the United States. It really wasn't close either, in terms of the electoral college. Before the 11 o'clock newscasts had hit the airwaves, it was apparent that even the large bounty of electoral votes awarded to California would make a difference. Trump had successfully engendered such a mixture of resentment, anger, hope, and passion from blue-collar workers in the

South, East, and Midwest – including in Jackson's native state of Indiana – that it kept red states as red and shifted swing states as equally red.

He started having that sinking, slinking feeling before the 11 p.m. news confirmed it: Donald Trump had defeated Hillary Clinton for the White House. Teddy forcefully turned off his television remote control in disgust. What ensued was a restless, sleepless, comfort-less night. He awoke to the sensational sunrise and hopes that it was all a nightmare of some sort. It was a nightmare, alright, but not of fictional variety. It was true, all true, and Teddy had to step outside just to make sense of it all.

He thought to himself, first in innermost thoughts, and then in audible whispers, as he slowly traipsed Market Street: *But the polls had her winning by ten to twelve points. The electoral college projections had her at over 400. And now they're saying she still won the popular vote by four million votes? How can this be? How could Americans elect such a narcissist, angry, incompetent, inexperienced man?*

Teddy stopped, realizing his rant to himself made him look like one of the many, mentally ill people he encountered on his sidewalk every day. He returned his thoughts inwardly. *This man openly invited Russia to hack our cyber-systems to dig up dirt on the Democratic Party. And he succeeded, even though Hillary was cleared of wrongdoing. And he's rewarded with a victory?!*

Even as these thoughts processed, Teddy was still struck by how the normally bustling downtown streets – with car stereos blaring and high heels clicking against asphalt and dogs yelping loudly – were so quiet. He had once visited Boston because it featured Fenway Park and was the birthplace, in the inner city of Roxbury, of his all-time favorite group, New Edition. Car horns blared incessantly in Beantown, and every time he heard a horn in San Diego, he'd think *Well at least it's quieter here than in Boston.* But this time that quietness held a creepy sensation for him, as if something was amiss. Did all of downtown San Diego, with its amalgam of black homeless dudes, white law school students, Latino gardeners, and other stereotypes personified feel as shocked as he?

He arrived to the Meshugga Shack, a converted trailer truck that was now a coffee shop with several tables and umbrellas sprawled about. On a gorgeous morning like this, it was a welcome place to enjoy some rays or haze with one's cup of joe. A tug came at his right elbow.

Teddy turned around. It was a grinning Murph, standing directly behind him.

"Wassup, Action Jackson?" Murph cordially greeted him.

"Hey, Murph, what's happening?" Teddy said as he leaned in for the typical man-hug – a clasping of hands, followed by a lean that's just shy of a hug, completed with a mutual pat on the back. Men in America, at least sports fans, and these two certainly fit that bill, had seen athletes increasingly do that for the past decade. It was now part of the American male body language, like standing asymmetrically in conversation or punctuating a point of agreement with a fist bump.

As they moved up in line, Murph offered to buy Teddy's coffee. "I got this, man," Murph insisted, handing the server his credit card, "today's a celebration."

"What?" asked Teddy, returning his crumpled ten-dollar bill back into his faded wallet.

"Trump, baby, I told you we'd win!" Murph explained giddily.

Teddy rolled his eyes and ordered a small cup of machiatta, extra cream, no sugar.

Murph continued, "Look, man, don't give me this crap that I'm racist. I voted for Obama twice – and he didn't do jack. My uncles work in steel mills in the Midwest and they've been unemployed forever. My healthcare costs are through the roof and there's *no way* I wanted that conniving liar Hillary Clinton in the White House. Trump ain't politically correct but he keeps it real, bro. I voted for him and I challenge any of these liberal bastards out here to challenge me on that!"

Murph was now a combination of post-election exulting and defiance. Teddy sipped his coffee as they eased away from the coffee shack. He needed to process these thoughts against his own simmering rage. It helped that he knew and liked Murph and wasn't hearing this rationale from some right-wing blowhard on Fox News.

Suddenly, a thought hit Teddy. "Murph, why are you down here so early anyway, man, don't you work in North County?"

Murph's countenance lowered. He responded, "Yeah, man, I do but Jenn asked if we could meet for breakfast today. Talk some things out. We've been having problems lately."

"Oh," said Teddy, knowing he was completely unsurprised.

Murph continued, "Anyway, I gotta bounce. I'll let you know how it goes. Trump, baby!"

They bumped Styrofoam cups of coffee and man-hugged in departure. Teddy chose to avoid looking at a nearby *San Diego Union-Tribune* newspaper for sale. His phone flashed a news notification from CNN: *Election protestors flood U.S. streets.* He was certain Murph would've called them idiots. His emotions ranged from proud to dejected to angry to forlorn. It was morning again in America.

"Look at the omelette on this menu! It's huge!" Murph exclaimed.

"Yeah, it's pretty big," said Jenn, seated across from him in a wood-paneled booth.

"Or as Trump would say, IT'S YUGE!" Murph chortled at his own joke.

They were at the Broken Yolk, a breakfast-all-day franchise nestled in the section of East Village that morphed into the Gaslamp Quarter, San Diego's older, more cosmopolitan, more touristy part of downtown. Though there were Broken Yolk replicates in other parts of the city, the downtown one still had a down-home feel that prevented it from feeling carbon-copied.

Murph was correct. The Broken Yolk had an omelette challenge, whereby if a customer ate a monstrous, two-pound omelette, with all the fixings of mushrooms and bell peppers and olives and such, they'd win an assortment of rewards: a free meal, a t-shirt, and of course the notoriety of having devoured such a ferocious meal. Jenn didn't even bother to look over the prizes. She knew the idea of even tackling such an egg-filled beast just sounded gross, plain and simple.

Truthfully, Murph wasn't swayed by the winnings either, nor the sumptuous allure of eating this bulging bastion of a breakfast. Even his Trump imitation, though he was supremely pleased at the victory, underscored what Murph was really feeling at this moment.

Nervousness.

Jenn had invited him to breakfast, ostensibly, to talk. This was usually a precursor, for couples who were struggling, to have "The Talk."

He also got a hint that, while he went big with his order of steak and eggs, her order was far less substantial. A breakfast roll and a small cup of coffee, black, slight cream. Jenn wasn't a full-fledged vegetarian but preferred not to eat eggs, bacon, or steak, or anything that involved killing animals. It drove Murph nuts.

Clearly Jenn had two n's and one mission: to get to the heart of the matter.

"Murph," she began, "we need to talk…"

Murph interjected, "Uh-oh, nothing good comes from 'we need to talk'."

Jenn calmly continued: "We've been dating for about nine months now. I mean, gash, I don't even know if I should call you my boyfriend. You never specifically asked me to be your girlfriend."

"Aw, baby," Murph cringed, "no one really does that anymore. It's so old-fashioned. I would hope you know by the stuff I do for you and the way I treat you that I really care about you. You're my girl."

"Well I'm old fashioned!" Jenn responded crossly.

The tone of her voice, as did many of their conversations recently, escalated quickly.

"Look, Jenn, whatever your problem is, I'm sure we can work it out."

"MY problem? MY problem?"

The server, Ignacio, came with the food, which abruptly silenced Jenn. "Gracias, Ignacio," Jenn said, which drew a derisive smirk from Murph.

She then resumed in a whisper that was really a yell: *My problem? What do you mean, MY problem?*

"Look, Jenn, I really care about you," Murph stated, picking up his knife and fork to attack the steak simultaneously, "but it's a little hard when someone else obviously has eyes for you."

"What? Who?" asked Jenn in rapid-fire succession.

"Come on," replied Murph, plunging into his New York T-bone, "I see the way Fernando looks at you. Clearly he likes you."

"Oh my gash, whatever," said Jenn, shaking her head and rolling her eyes. "And so what if he does? I'm with YOU. You've never formally asked me to be your girlfriend, but I'm with you."

"Well, that's questionable too," said Murph, between chews, "I mean, you spend half your time with this group of friends you didn't even know last Christmas. Now they're your best buds, your constant companions."

"And what's wrong with that?" Her face now matched the ruddy exterior of the red t-shirt and cap she was wearing on this day. Jenn was still jobless so every day was casual attire.

"I'm just sayin', look, ok, let me be frank here," said Murph, putting down his utensils. "You've had a rough year. I could never understand what it's like to lose your mother and job in the same year. And I'm glad you have friends that are supportive but I think these guys have made you a little, uh..."

"What?"

"SOFT, ok? They've made you soft." The verb blurted out of Murph's mouth like word-vomit, forcefully and quickly.

"Oh my goodness, you gatta be kidding me," replied Jenn, throwing her napkin on the table for no good reason except to express disgust.

Murph wasn't done. "Look, hear me out. Why did Trump resonate with so many people? Because Obama made us SOFT, Jennifer, especially our generation. We've become these snowflakes that are, like, scared of adversity and criticism and hard times."

Jenn's face was a combination of confusion and anger. Furrowing her eyebrows, she asked, "What the heck does our relationship have to do with PALITICS?"

"Hear me out, now, hear me out," Murph continued. Both of his hands were extended now, as he was growing more emphatic. "These friends of yours, Jenn, they're good people but did they really help you much? You lost your mom and your job. And you lost it. Mentally, you lost it. You haven't had ambition or drive. I mean, look at you, unemployed for months now and you're not really looking hard. And is this Wolfpack driving you to start a new career? No! They hug you, they cry with you, they tell you everything's going to be ok."

Jenn folded her arms. "And how else should they have responded?" she asked.

Murph quickly answered, "By pushing you. By pushing you to be better and start over, by pushing you to overcome your sadness. Look, Jenn, all I'm saying is you are a bright and beautiful girl. And we live in a gorgeous city with gorgeous weather. I wanna see you get back on track. All I'm saying is lean on me. I may not be as sensitive or coddling as your friends, but I'll get you back on track. Just trust me."

Jenn remained silent for a moment. Ignacio returned to offer more coffee but she declined. She then leaned in across the table and said: "You know, Murph, all my life I've been wrapped up in other people. My jab. My mother and her approval. My friends. Even my boyfriends. I don't think the answer is trusting in you, or this city, or even in my friends. I think it's time I look at ALL my options. I need to take care of me."

"Well, w-w-what does that mean?" asked a perplexed Murph.

Jenn stood up. She pulled a 20-dollar bill from her brown, leather purse and tossed it onto the table.

"It means," she said, "you and me are like your steak. Stick a fork in us. We're done."

With that she strode away, forcefully yet gracefully, opening the doors to the outward city and to her destiny.

Friendsgiving

Her pink sneakers pounded the East Village asphalt. Pink versus pavement. Bea Feliz's sneakers were an immediate statement of femininity, a declaration of awareness of breast cancer, and a show of toughness given the obvious wear and tear these running shoes had endured.

It was Thanksgiving morning. Like hundreds of millions of other Americans, Beatriz had the same afternoon agenda: football and feasting. But before she was going to dig into an assortment of turkey, ham, casserole, salad, cranberry sauce, biscuits, and pies – traditionally pumpkin though she preferred cherry – she wanted to make sure she first got in a good run.

Her father had taken the kids to St. Vincent de Paul's Village, a downtown homeless shelter on 14th Street and Imperial Avenue, to feed those less fortunate. It was something they used to do with Bea as a teenager, before returning home to a Thanksgiving meal prepared solely by her mother. Really, it was two meals because in addition to the American custom of turkey and stuffing and corn, there were also homemade Mexican tamales. This was a tradition repeated at Christmas, save for replacing the turkey with a juicy ham. But tamales, there were always tamales.

There was also the Dallas Cowboys, a tradition as evergreen as the food itself. Whether the family brood included - via marriage, birth, death, and everything in between - grandparents, siblings, cousins, college roommates, and occasionally neighbors having fallen on hard times, the Cowboys were never absent. Danny White, Ed "Too Tall" Jones, Herschel Walker, Troy Aikman, Emmitt Smith, Michael Irvin, Tony Romo, and now Dak Prescott and Ezekiel Elliott – the Cowboys were annual guests in Bea's Thanksgiving Day household.

She even identified certain holiday memories by prompts such as: *Thanksgiving Day 1992; you know, the one where it snowed in Dallas and*

Leon Lett cost the Cowboys the game by sliding into, and touching, a live kick. Oh, and that was the day cousin Martin proposed to Adriana and they lived happily ever after.

As she completed her late-morning jog, the skies a steely gray and brown leaves scattered throughout the sidewalks as she deeply ingested the brisk air, she waved hello to the doorman guarding her brownstone. She thought perhaps her Papa would be back with the kids. For certain Mama would be in the kitchen, furiously preparing the turkey *and* tamales, looking anguished in every moment but then shooing away all help, unless it was offered by any female family members. Beatriz hated that.

The family schedule was the same every year. Eat by noon, so that by the time the Cowboys came on CBS at 1:30, it was time for burping, dessert, tryptophan-induced naps, or perhaps all three.

Bea opened the door and removed her ear buds. She expected to hear the sounds of her mother rattling in the kitchen and the morning game – always the Detroit Lions versus a Green Bay, or Chicago, or some other Midwest mauler – blaring in the living room. She felt the need to remind her mom that she wasn't going to eat as much as usual, because her pal Fernando was hosting a "Friendsgiving" – a meal for any friends without significant others, spouses, or family in the area. Beatriz had plenty of family, plus her kids, but the divorce with Jose was ongoing. So she was going to treat the kids, whom she and Jose were still in a custody battle over, to two meals, her mom and Fernando's later that afternoon.

What she didn't expect was this: her parents, seated at the dining room table, with an unexpected guest: Jose.

Her mind flashed to various *Star Wars* scenes where such an ambush called for the famous line of: "It's a trap!"

"Jose!" Bea was breathless from both the jog and surprise visitation. "What are you…..Ma, what is he doing here?"

Jose stood up and greeted Beatriz with a peck on the cheek, which she half-heartedly accepted. He intoned in a thick Spanish accent, "Beatriz, don't worry. I asked your parents if I could come over. I have, uh, some things to propose."

She looked at her son and daughter in the hallway and instructed them to go into their bedrooms. Amid their moans of protest, she quickly turned to Jose and said, "Well you better make it quick because after eating here I'm gonna take the kids to a friend's dinner."

"You mean your silly little friend Fernandito?" Jose asked mockingly.

Bea was clearly annoyed at Jose already and at her parents for communicating with him beforehand to coordinate this…this ambush? This summit? This intervention?

She asked, "Jose, what do you want? What could you possibly be proposing?"

"Beatriz," he said slowly and gently, "I would like for us to have one complete Thanksgiving meal together. As a family. And…I would like to end the divorce proceedings. I've left her, Bea. I want to be with you."

The words hit Bea like a bucket of ice water. Two summers ago, she allowed her colleagues to drench her with a freezing bucket of H2O as part of the "Ice Bucket Challenge" that rampaged across America in the name of raising funds and awareness for cognitive and neurological diseases. Yeah, it felt just like that.

What amazed Bea was as soon as Jose uttered those words – "I want to be with you" – she could see from the corner of her eye that Papa was smiling and Mama was weeping joyfully and even let out an emotional "*Ayyy!*" She could also see her kids peeking through a sliver of their bedroom doorway. All it took was one stern expression from Bea, with an angry brow and pursed lips, for the kiddos to scramble back in. Her sweat had dried from the workout but she suddenly felt flush.

Here was the man of her dreams, who had broken her heart, and then turned everything into a nightmare by saying he wanted full custody. And now he wanted her back? Just like that? After cheating on her?

Another sensation simultaneously hit Beatriz, an audible one. It was her cell phone buzzing rapidly, usually an indication her Wolfpack was exchanging text messages. She glanced at her phone, partially out of curiosity and partially out of annoyance toward her parents and estranged husband.

As she suspected, her posse was texting back and forth about that afternoon's Friendsgiving meal at Fernando's. She scrolled quickly and read at a glance:

Fernando was providing turkey, salad, and mashed potatoes. But please bring wine.

Jenn was supplying a healthy salad, organic casserole, and wine.

Teddy said he'd bring some pies and a couple ladies. The group shot down the latter.

Beatriz, a query went out, are you still bringing corn and cranberry sauce and wine? She quickly responded with a thumbs-up emoji.

And where was Liz? Had anyone heard from Liz?

Another flurry of texts went out with everyone noting they hadn't heard from Liz.

"Beatriz, mija," her mother walked slowly toward her, "please, put your phone down for just a moment."

When Bea set her cellular device down on a nearby glass coffee table, her mother continued. "Mija, you have a great opportunity here. To keep your family together. To show your kids the power of forgiveness. Don't do it for us, my dear, do it for the kids. They're in the Montessori School now and they're growing up so fast. Give them a stable environment."

"I love them," added Jose, "and I love you. All I want is to make you happy."

"Yes, dear," her father suddenly said, stroking his salt-and-pepper mustache, "we all just want to make you happy."

Bea Feliz thought about her life in one, instant snapshot. Taking a cursory, yet panoramic, view of the brownstone, she saw instant mementos of her life. Framed pictures of college graduation. Eight-by-ten glossies of her kids. Rosary beads acquired by her mother. She glanced at her pink sneakers and how they had carried her through two full marathons, three half-marathons, and a slew of 5 and 10k races. Nearby was a Bible and a collection of DVD's of female comedians like Amy Schumer and Margaret Cho.

She quietly picked up her cell phone again and saw a new thread had begun. Everyone was guessing where Liz was. The suggestions:

She was out buying all the wine in the city.

She was poisoning Trump's turkey.

She was leading a protest march somewhere but would be done by dinner.

Bea set her phone down again and creased the corners of her lips into a slight smile. The more she thought about things, the more she smiled.

"Guys," she addressed both her parents and Jose. "I am happy. I'm happy with my life. I'm happy with my career. I'm happy being apart from this cheating bastard."

Her mother was aghast. Bea continued: "I'm VERY happy with my friends. And after I eat a little bit here, I'm going to go join them. Now if you'll excuse me, I need to jump in the shower."

Everything at Fernando Guzman's Thanksgiving dinner was over the top. He festooned his condo with cornucopia baskets and pumpkins and paper-machete napkins and anything that hinted at Turkey Day or autumn or both. The food was an extravagant assortment of turkey and ham and green bean casserole salad with walnuts on top and creamy mashed potatoes and corn and salads – one with feta cheese and one without – and biscuits and cranberry sauce and so much more. His guests openly wondered why Freddy had them bring anything, though he emphasized that all the fixins' – plus the separate counter for pies and cakes and creamy desserts - were a combination of his cooking, with assistance from Jenn, plus contributions from each guest. His ex-fiancee Katie McDonald would've never liked having this many decorations or people in the apartment, which was a plus of her being an ex.

Especially abundant was the wine. Oh how it flowed. Everyone brought some, save for Teddy, who brought some pies and had largely limited his alcohol intake since the DUI arrest. He also brought no dates, which surprised everyone but seemingly left Teddy feeling fairly fulfilled. "Let's eat and watch football, fam!" he hollered.

Beatriz came, having shorn her track suit for jeans and a snug black sweater, and brought her two kids. Jenn was present, minus Murph, of which most of the group was just finding out about the breakup, so his absence was largely greeted with sounds of *Awwwwww!* Two co-workers of Fernando – one from Mexico and the other from Ohio – came because they had no family in the area.

As Fernando started tallying bodies and whisper-shouting his head count, he stopped suddenly and asked aloud, "You guys, where's Liz? She has not responded to one text all day."

Everyone shrugged and resumed pouring wine.

For the next three hours, consumption was the operative word. Food was gorged on. Wine was poured liberally and downed quickly – everyone could either walk back to their East Village abode or take an Uber home. Cowboys football was watched, by Beatriz, carefully, vigorously, and loudly, and the whole group couldn't help but be enthralled when Dallas won in the final minute.

Bea was so charged up she stood in the center of the room, punched the air with her right fist, and exultantly shouted, "How 'Bout Them Cowboys?!"

Everyone raised their glasses and cheered, even if for no other reason than to support the small but sassy Cowboys fanatic.

All, except one.

"Booooooooo!"

Every head swiveled to the lone voice standing in the doorway. The room fell silent.

It was Murph, Jenn's newly estranged boyfriend. He had walked in, among the hubbub, holding a six-pack of Stone Ale Brewery pale ale beer.

"Hi everyone. Hello, Jennifer." Murph appeared slightly nervous but also seemed to relish the grand entry.

Jenn was stunned. "Murph. Wha-…how….how?"

"How did I know you were here?" he asked rhetorically. "I read Liz's post on Facebook that she was planning on coming to Fernando's party but that she needed to get really hammered first because she was sad."

"What?" Beatriz was shaken by this news and scrolled through her Facebook immediately.

Everyone looked at each other in shock but Murph didn't want to lose the momentum. "Jenn, I love you," he said, "and you drive me crazy sometimes but…"

He took off his red MAKE AMERICA GREAT AGAIN and held it to his chest. "But I know we can work things out. I know you didn't mean those words. I'm willing to give this one more chance, if you are."

Jenn was torn. She knew Murph's words sounded cocky but were somehow sincere. She arose from the couch. Murph set his cap down on a bookcase.

A male voice boomed, "No!"

Everyone's heads swiveled in the opposite direction. It was Fernando.

"Jennifer, you shouldn't go back to him," he said stridently. "This man doesn't appreciate you or value you or care about all the little things that make you so great."

Murph feigned indignation. "Oh what? Puh-leeze."

He stepped toward Fernando. Teddy blocked Murph's body and stonewalled him.

Fernando continued: "Jenn, you should maintain some dignity and pride, and I know the wine is helping me right now, but I believe this. You deserve a man that understands your causes, and what makes you happy, and what makes you feel pain too. You deserve someone who appreciates you. You deserve...me, Jenn. I'm nothing special, I'm a nobody...but...but...but I love you."

The room occupants gasped.

Jenn burst into tears and ran into a bathroom.

Beatriz suddenly chimed in, "You guys, I don't mean to interrupt this episode of *Days of our Lives* here. But Liz wrote all these posts and seems really distraught. And, oh my goodness, she just posted this five minutes ago."

"What's it say?" asked Fernando.

Bea covered her mouth with her hand and then breathlessly read it aloud: I WANT TO KILL MYSELF.

With that everyone jumped up from couches and recliners and every voice spoke at once.

"Well let's not just stand here, knuckleheads," said Murph, "Beatriz, go get Jenn. Freddy, call 911. Let's go to her place RIGHT NOW!"

It was a fire drill of calamitous proportions, everyone bouncing into each other like ants. Fernando called 911 and described the situation. Beatriz pulled Jenn out of the latrine and all stoves, lights, and appliances were shut off. They poured out of the apartment quickly. Teddy grabbed the unattended MAKE AMERICA GREAT AGAIN and threw it in the trash.

Another post suddenly appeared:

SO DRUNK, SO SAD, I MISS YOU KRIS, I HAVE CANCER, NO REASON TO LIVE. I WANT TO KILL MYSELF.

Chapter 10

New Beginnings

Seeing Liz's ominous Facebook posts interrupted all Friendsgiving feasting, football watching, arguments, and declarations of love. Liz was the only member of the crew who didn't live in East Village, which was as inconvenient as the fact that everyone had spent all afternoon not turning water into wine, but rather drinking wine like it was water. They hustled downstairs and ordered multiple Ubers to transport them to the beach area.

Murph got Liz's address from Beatriz, which was essential for the Ubers and the 9-1-1 call that sent a paramedic directly to Liz's apartment. They didn't know what she was doing to herself, or what she *might* do, but the social media posts were clearly a cry for help. It was better to call paramedics and not take any chances.

Good thing they did. The paramedics burst through the door and Liz was laying on her couch. Bottles of beer and hard liquor were strewn everywhere. She was half-comatose and already entering into a slumber. Her cell phone was on the ground next to the couch, adjacent to an unmarked bottle of pills.

Beatriz gasped and then ordered her two kids to stay in the hallway. Jenn commenced crying. The medics acted quickly, propping her head up. *She has a pulse but we have to prevent her from choking. Everyone stand back,* they shouted.

Murph and Freddy, virtual enemies less than a half hour ago, became unspoken comrades in holding everyone back from entering the living room. Teddy took the kids' hands and escorted them to the lobby so Gabby and Max wouldn't see or hear this rather traumatic ugliness.

The workers pumped Liz's stomach. *ONE, TWO, THREE, PUMP! ONE, TWO, THREE, PUMP!*

It all came out. The Budweiser, the Heineken, the Corona, the Johnny Walker, the bourbon, the scotch. Every bottle clinking at their feet was now coming out in regurgitated, soupy, liquid, smelly form. Liz must have anticipated this could be an end result because she placed a cylindrical trash can next to her sofa. It was now a puke bucket and it was filling up fast.

Hold her head firm now, don't let her wobble, get it all out. It all came out. The sadness. The pain. The regret over letting her parents down by not doing better in school or securing a good, full-time job. The fear that engulfed her when the doctors confirmed there was cancer and radiation would soon begin. The agony when Kris was also overtaken by fear, and just couldn't handle it, plus the mounting medical bills, and just took off. All that was left was a note one morning: *Please know I'll always love you. I just need to step away for now. I'm sorry.*

What did that mean? Was stepping away a temporary or permanent move? It was painfully unclear but absolutely caused Liz Wong to feel angry, betrayed, hurt, and lonely, and all that was coming out. Wretch after violent wretch, it was all coming out. *Alcohol poisoning*, they said, making it all sound so simple, the same type of activity you can find in a freshman dorm or belligerent bachelor party on any given Saturday night. But it was so much more. As they wheeled Liz out onto a stretcher, and into an ambulance, sirens wailing, lights blaring, half of the Wolfpack climbing aboard and the other half following in a Lyft, and heading to a hospital, the truth was evident: Liz had clearly tried to end her life.

The day after Thanksgiving, while most people were shopping, watching college football, eating leftover turkey sandwiches crammed with cranberry sauce and mayonnaise and mustard, or hanging up Christmas lights, the Wolfpack was gathered around a hospital bed. Nationally it was Black Friday but for them it was a Good Friday – their friend Liz was still alive.

Stubbornly clamoring "I'm fine!" she tried unsuccessfully to get the hospital to discharge her but they rejected her rancor-filled requests. Liz was so severely dehydrated they attached intravenous fluids into her and wanted to monitor her progress. The doctors also wanted her to speak to a staff psychologist to gauge her mental stability. Additionally, given her ongoing radiation treatments, Liz was in a rather fragile physical state overall.

Her friends were glad the hospital was not giving in to her rants and encircled her bed. It was Fernando, who did bring a heaping plate of food from his party; Beatriz, who left her kids at home; Teddy; and Jenn. Murph elected not to come, given the tension between he and Fernando, and just to give Jenn some space. Assuredly, although their primary focus was on Liz, both Bea and Jenn had their minds swimming after their estranged lovers had made Thanksgiving Day pleas for reconciliation. Were they turkeys or treats?

"You know what's cool about the day after Thanksgiving?" Liz mused drowsily, "Today is when all the Christmas movies start playing on TV."

"And the best one," dove in Fernando, "is *Love Actually*."

"No way, man," replied Teddy, "it's *Bad Santa*. One AND two."

"You're both nuts," said Jenn, "it's totally *Elf*."

"What about *Christmas Story*?"

The question silenced the room. It was a new voice.

An unexpected voice. A soft one that still reverberated throughout the dimly light and sparsely decorated surroundings.

Everyone turned around. Liz looked up. She was stunned but recognized the soft intonation immediately.

It was her runaway lover. Kris.

No one in the group knew what to say to her.

Another Chance

"I saw your posts yesterday," she said quietly, "and I was really worried. Then I found out you were hospitalized and did some digging around until I found out you were here."

Compared to the rest of the group in their day-off jeans and sweatshirts representing Notre Dame, San Diego State, USC, and the like, Kris was immaculately dressed. She wore a tight-fitting black dress that hugged every curve and was adorned with a purple sash. Her black high heels touched the floor crisply and her flowing auburn-colored hair flowed past her stunning gold necklace and tiny shoulders.

She looked luminous.

"Uh, maybe we should give you two a minute," said Jenn.

"Good idea," concurred Fernando.

The Wolfpack started shuffling past Kris when Teddy extended his right hand and smiled. "Teddy Jackson, pleasure to meet you. Some call me Action Jackson."

"Teddy!" exclaimed Beatriz. "GET over here!"

She pointed to the doorway and Teddy dutifully followed. Within five seconds the room had cleared and there they were, Kris and Liz. Just like an action movie which inevitably pits the two leading characters into a showdown, this was it. This was the long-awaited climax.

There was momentarily silence.

Then they both started to talk. And stopped. And tripped over the awkwardness. And then Kris re-started more forcibly.

"I'm sorry."

Liz had waited agonizingly for months for those words. Hearing them provided some salve but her heart was still racing and her mind was still spinning.

Kris continued. "I freaked out, ok? I've always gotten on you for not being more responsible or for not being a better planner. And then your illness hit. And bills started piling up. And I freaked, ok? I freaked. I lost my father to cancer. I just...I just...I just didn't want to go through that again."

"So now what?" asked Liz with tears in her eyes.

"I wanna do better, Liz, I wanna do better," said Kris, clutching Liz's right wrist, which still had the IV tube going through it. "And when all this happened last night, and you wound up here, I got a real taste of the possibility of losing you...forever."

"So?" Liz inquired with both curiosity and defiance.

"So...I want us to get back together."

They were the words Liz yearned and dreaded to hear.

She closed her eyes. A tear rolled down her flushed face.

One Year Later

The phone rang and rang, yet went unanswered. Text messages were unreturned and unreciprocated.

After returning to Liz's hospital room to continue their visit – and finding her mostly tight-lipped about Kris's sudden appearance – the Wolfpack went their separate ways for the afternoon.

Jenn figured this was a good opportunity to resume her conversation with Fernando about his not-entirely-surprising-yet-still-stunning declaration of love for her at his dinner the night before. Everything went haywire after that but a good night's sleep, plus knowing Liz was stable, put Jenn in a much better state of mind.

So after everyone dispersed in mid-afternoon, she reached out to Fernando, but to no avail. That was how Liz's breakdown began too, with silence followed by an ultimate alcohol-infused meltdown. Jenn knew Fernando would never quite go to those extremes, based on what he often cited as his father instilling a strong sense of responsibility and accountability within him. But she took no chances, finally heading straight to his residence.

She found him. She knew *where* to find him.

The rooftop view revealed an exploding sunset. The air was still. Barely a car horn could be heard on the streets below, although as was always the case in East Village, dogs barked and yelped and pitter-pattered their paws as they jogged alongside their owners.

"How did you know where to find me?" Fernando asked, with a smirk.

"This is where you go to think," replied Jenn.

"No, this is where *Katie* used to go to think," he said. "I would follow her up here. Ya' know, it was almost one year ago she and I threw a Christmas party, and she came up to this rooftop to think and stew and eventually tell me she was unhappy."

"Well, did you listen?" Jenn asked, edging closer to him.

"No," Fernando said flatly, "I basically stayed in denial. I was convinced I did all the textbook things a boyfriend or fiancée should do. Maybe if I listened better she and I would still be together."

"Oh," said Jenn softly.

Fernando continued. "But you know what, Jennifer? That's not what bothers me. Losing her is not what bothers me. What bothers me is here we are, a year later, and everyone has taken a good, hard look in the mirror and made adjustments to their lives. All of us, we've all lost something, but everyone's made adjustments. Teddy doesn't need to be around women all the time, or be this big celebrity, and he's even got some job interviews lined up. Bea is more of an independent woman, and I don't know if she'll get back with Jose, but I'll tell you what, whatever she decides won't be out of fear or parental pressure. And I'm sure blacking out last night straightened up Liz, she knows she can't depend on another person for happiness now. And you, hey, you broke up with Murph. You're, like, the poster child for independence now."

Jenn laughed, then asked, "And what about you, *Señor* Fernando Guzman? You lost something big this year too. Did it change you?"

Fernando looked out at the rooftop view of the city, lights beginning to shimmer like emerging constellations, and wistfully replied, "I don't know. I don't know if I've changed. I mean, I *think* I've changed, but if Katie hadn't left me, would I have changed? Or would I still be this smothering dude who's afraid to let down his girlfriend or parents or boss or friends? Like, I love seeing people be happy, but who am I? Who am I, Jenn?"

Jenn let out a deep breath and then said, "Well, I don't know. I mean, it's a fair question, but one only you can answer. Are you this person that's changed because you lost love? Or did losing love help you re-discover who you *really* are? Do we ever really change or do we evolve, ya' know, into the real person we are?"

Fernando put his arm around Jenn's shoulders, partially in unity and partly because it was getting chilly. He said, "I feel….like I need to reinvent myself. Not a fake, superficial type of re-inventing but a discovery of who I really am. When I lost Katie, I felt like I lost *everything*. Now I'm ready to just….find myself."

New Year's Day

It was New Year's Day 2017.

The January 1st mid-afternoon sunshine was poking through the otherwise bleak haze.

The air was quiet with recovery, the previous night a memory of streamers, champagne, confetti, and toasts for a prosperous future.

The Wolfpack had rung in the New Year together – predictably, at Bub's in the East Village – but what seemingly mattered more was their get-together the next day.

No one was hung over. No one was wallowing in despair or regret.

At half past noon they were assembled, not in the East Village, but in a tidy park in Coronado, which was connected to downtown via the Coronado Bay Bridge.

Though they were not hung over, most of the crew was still pretty tired, including Teddy, who groggily asked, "Why are we here so early in the day on this island?"

"I don't consider it an island," replied Liz, "really it's a peninsula."

"But they call themselves an island," interjected Beatriz.

Liz shot back, "I don't care if they call themselves a volcano, it's not an island. An island is, like, stand-alone and surrounded by water. *This* place has one strand of land connecting it to the city."

"Yes, the Silver Strand," offered Fernando, "look, I don't care if it's an island, peninsula, or Teddy's backyard."

Everyone laughed. Fernando continued: "We just wanted everyone together one last time. You know we leave today for Vegas. And, you know, we wanted to get one last group picture. Why not have beautiful Coronado as the backdrop?"

Jose spoke up. "Here, let me take the picture. You guys all get together."

Beatriz smiled at her estranged-but-still-husband.

It had been a whirlwind month. She decided to accept his proposal to stay together, but only on the condition they undergo marriage counseling. She was a feminist and her black t-shirt with white lettering belied that: THE FUTURE IS FEMALE. Many of her friends didn't understand how she could take back an admitted cheater. Truthfully she didn't even consider doing so until she was convinced there was no other woman. But being a feminist wasn't about disobeying one's parents or seeking revenge against a wayward lover. It was about *choice* and she chose – *she chose*, not her parents or friends or Latino custom or peer pressure – to forgive Jose. Their marriage was going to survive.

Now would her Cowboys survive in the playoffs?

Conversely, Liz said no to Kris. Her lover had deserted her in a time of need. As couples grow more serious, there are more serious and frequent types of need. If Kris panicked at the first hint of cancer, what if Liz worsened? Or what if Liz got better? Eventually another crisis or trauma or moment of need would arise. Kris lost that trust and Liz lost that relationship, but gained something greater: inner strength.

Teddy was dressed down, which for him were Bermuda shorts and sandals, but that was ok. He didn't have anyone to impress. He didn't have a date lined up for that day or night. He *did* have an interview scheduled for the following week for a sports marketing agency that specialized in events that benefitted poor communities. He was excited about that. Teddy realized it wasn't women or Obama or Trump or sports teams or celebrity status that was in charge of his happiness. It was him.

"Alright, everyone, get together," called out Jose, "three, two, and one..."

He pressed the photo button on Fernando's phone and then remarked, "I'm not gonna take pictures with everyone's phones. Freddy can send it to all you guys."

"He's right," Fernando said, smiling at Jenn. "We've got a long drive to Las Vegas. We'll send this pic to you guys on the way."

Fernando and Jenn with two n's were moving to Vegas together, seeking new employment, residence, and a future. He was the leader of the Wolfpack but in a real wolfpack, the true leader runs behind the group. That would be someone else's responsibility now.

She was ready for change. He was ready to find himself. They knew both would be accomplished at each other's side.

A New Year awaited. *Wolfpack hoooooowl.*

Printed in the United States
By Bookmasters